"Can't you see how wrong I am for you, Rob?"

Micah pleaded. "If you cared for me, you wouldn't ask me any more questions...."

Rob caught up with her in a few long strides. "I do care about you," he said as he turned her to face him, "and nothing that's happened in the past will change that. But I want to know the truth, Micah. I want to understand."

"You can't understand. Unless you've lived it, you can't know what it's like." With pleading eyes, she stared into the stormy depths of his gaze. "Please, Rob..."

"You trust me with today, but not with yesterday? Is that it?"

"If I wanted my past to be part of my life, I would have stayed in California. But I'm not there—I'm here, with you." She paused. "And this is where I want to be...for now. Don't ask for more."

KATHRYN ALEXANDER

loves to write, and the publication of her first book, *The Reluctant Bride,* is the realization of a dream, an answer to a prayer and proof that a book can be written piecemeal, in small portions of time.

She writes inspirational romance because, having been a Christian for many years, incorporating the element of faith in the Lord into a romantic story line seemed like a lovely and appropriate idea. After all, in a society where love for a lifetime is difficult to find, imagine discovering it, unexpectedly, as a gift sent from God.

Married to Kelly, her own personal love of a lifetime, Kathryn and her husband have one son, John, who is the proud owner of the family's two housepests (not a typo), Herbie the cat and Copper the dog.

Kathryn and her family have been members of their church for nearly five years, where she co-teaches a Sunday school class of active two-year-olds. She is now a stay-at-home mom who writes between carpooling, baby-sitting and applying bandages, when necessary.

The Reluctant Bride

Kathryn Alexander

Love Inspired™

Published by Steeple Hill Books™

STEEPLE HILL BOOKS

Steeple
Hill™

ISBN 0-373-87018-3

THE RELUCTANT BRIDE

Printed in U.S.A.

The Lord is my shepherd; I shall not want.
—*Psalms* 23:1

To my husband, Kelly, who continues to give me the happiest years of my life (may there be many more!), and to our son, John, for his many hours of playing cars on the library floor close to the word processor while I typed my first book.

Chapter One

"**I** thought you said Michael Shepherd was here." The dark-haired attorney directed his half statement, half question to the receptionist, but his eyes lingered on the only person seated in the lobby: a young, pretty woman with auburn curls pushed casually over her shoulder, and her nose buried in a magazine. She looked up at the mention of the name.

"And this," the lawyer stated matter-of-factly, "is definitely not a Michael."

"It's Micah Shepherd," she explained, returning the magazine to the coffee table and rising from her chair. "M-I-C-A-H."

A darkening gaze surveyed her briefly. "Witness to the Winslow accident?"

"Yes," Micah responded. "I received a letter asking me to come in to answer a few questions."

"Yes, I sent the letter. I'm Rob Granston." He smiled as he shook the slender hand Micah extended toward him.

Rob Granston appeared much like Micah's friend Carole had described. Tall, yes, just as Micah needed to match her own height of five-eight, and his eyes were the gentle blue Carole had mentioned. His hair, coal black, looked soft and fine, but it was that wide, welcoming smile that his mouth curved into so easily that concerned Micah the most. Micah had come to the law offices today only because she felt it was her duty as a citizen. She had no intention of falling for this guy, no matter how "right" her friend claimed he would be for her.

"My client and I appreciate your taking the time to come in. Not everyone agrees to be interviewed when they're named as a witness to an automobile accident," Rob stated.

"I think it's my responsibility to tell you what I know about it. Will Mrs. Winslow be here this afternoon?" Micah asked.

"No, she's been hospitalized with back injuries," he responded as he directed her down a hallway. "First door to your left," he instructed, and they entered a large office decorated in deep, almost oppressive hues of brown and rust, with bulky furniture strategically placed throughout the room. Accustomed to the brightly colored, open spaces of a classroom, Micah found her surroundings slightly overwhelming.

"I apologize for the mix-up about your name. I believe the letter I sent was mistakenly addressed to 'Michael' Shepherd,'' Rob noted. "When Mrs. Winslow gave us the information, there was obviously some misunderstanding."

"It's all right," Micah replied. "When you have an unusual name like mine, you get used to that."

"I do need to ask a few questions. Please, have a seat, Miss Shepherd. It is 'Miss'?" Rob watched her sit down in the leather chair nearest the desk.

"Yes," Micah said with slight hesitation. "It is." She placed her small canvas handbag on the floor and silently prayed this meeting would not last long.

Rob took a seat behind his desk and from the clutter off to the side, he pulled a legal pad, the Winslow file and a pen. Looking up, he found Micah staring out the window.

"Twentieth floor," she commented.

"Yes." Rob glanced toward the window that had captured Micah's attention. "The view is the best thing about this office."

"The skyline is beautiful," she remarked, "but this room is so—" She stopped and looked toward his curious gaze. How did she manage to make such blunders?

"Dark? Dreary?" he suggested.

"Well, yes, but—"

"That's okay," he interrupted, the corners of his mouth lifting in genuine amusement. "I've thought the same thing many times. We're planning to re-decorate soon.''

Micah smiled, too, a smile of relief.

"Go ahead. Take a look.'' Rob nodded toward the glass and leaned back in his chair.

She rose from her seat and approached the window where she scanned the scenery below. It was a beautiful spring day the view encompassed—a view of the capital city in which she had lived for the past two winters, gray and icy, and two pleasant springs, summers and autumns. Surveying the variety of structures on the other side of the glass, she commented, "This would make a great painting."

"Are you an artist?"

"Yes," Micah said, "but it's my substitute teaching that pays the bills." She paused. "I've been in high-rise buildings in downtown Columbus, but I've never seen a lovelier view than this."

"Neither have I," came Rob's response, low and disturbing.

Micah turned, her green eyes colliding with a warm, interested blue gaze that had not been focused on the Ohio skyline. Clearing her throat nervously, she returned to her chair. "I guess we have an accident to discuss."

"There's no hurry," Rob replied, studying the faintly freckled face of the woman seated across from him. "You're my last appointment for the day."

"I really don't think I'll be much help to you,"

Micah began. "I'm sure you'd like to have a good witness for a P.I. case like this, but—"

"You said 'P.I.' You're familiar with personal injury cases?"

"A little." Micah hesitated. Two blunders in five minutes. Maybe she could break her own foolish record. All she longed for now was the conclusion of this interview and an open door. "I told Mrs. Winslow when she took my name and number the night of the accident that I wouldn't be a good witness."

Turning a pen over and over in his hands, Rob asked, "What makes you less than a good witness?" Then he smiled. Almost.

"A witness has to actually *see* something to be called a witness, and I didn't see anything." Micah looked down at her off-white cotton slacks and the multicolored striped shirt of neutral shades. Carole was right, she realized. This outfit was all wrong. With this guy she needed sweats and a good pair of running shoes.

"Mrs. Winslow seems to think you saw everything."

"You see, I was pulling out of the supermarket parking lot when I saw that big yellow car of Mrs. Winslow's going west on the street in front of the store. There was another car coming—"

"Going east?"

"Yes, and just as they approached each other, I sneezed." Micah shrugged. "Of course, my eyes shut for a moment, and when I looked up, the two cars had already crashed.''

Rob's mouth curved into that smile Micah liked far more than she wanted to admit. He scribbled something on the legal pad in front of him. ''Sneezing would have closed your eyes for only a second. Surely you saw something that—''

''But it happened several times. I'd purchased a mixed bouquet in the store's floral shop that night, and I guess I was allergic to some of the flowers.''

''What kind?''

''Carnations, daisies…I don't recall exactly.'' Micah frowned. ''Why?''

''Just curious,'' Rob responded quietly. ''You did speak with Mrs. Winslow that night. Did you explain any of this to her?''

''I tried to tell her. I usually shop for groceries on Thursday evenings and so does Mrs. Winslow. I didn't even know her name until the night of the wreck, but I would recognize her big yellow car anywhere. I always get out of her way.''

Rob leaned back in his chair. ''Get out of her way?'' The humor vanished.

''Yes,'' Micah replied. ''She drives like a maniac. That's why I wanted to come in for this appointment, to tell you how dangerous her driving is.''

Rob folded his hands together. ''I'm beginning to see why you are less than a good witness.''

''I'm sorry, Mr. Granston. It would highly surprise me to find out that the accident was *not* Mrs.

Winslow's fault. Anyone who drives as badly as she does should have their license revoked. Maybe you could do something about—"

"Miss Shepherd," Rob said, "my client is in the hospital with back injuries that may prove to be serious. We're not here to discuss the revocation of her driver's license."

But Micah persisted. Mrs. Winslow's driving ability, or the lack thereof, was mainly what had prompted her to make this appointment today. That, and her own curiosity. What made this stranger the perfect man for her, as her friend had proclaimed at least a dozen times? "But you're in a position to do something about this," she insisted. "Trying to win a case against the other driver, undoubtedly the victim here, isn't fair. Now that you know how badly Mrs. Winslow drives, maybe you could talk to her."

Rob stood up, bringing Micah's plea to an abrupt end. She was being dismissed, and she knew it.

"Thank you for coming, Miss Shepherd. I do appreciate your time and your honesty."

"I *am* being honest. Mrs. Winslow is dangerous behind the wheel of a car, and you'd be doing the public a great service by keeping her off the road."

"I'll take your comments into consideration," he said calmly.

Micah did not like attorneys. None of them. And she wondered now why she had ever agreed to meet with this one. The clock on the wall behind her chimed, and Micah glanced down at her watch.

"My bus," she said. "I must go or I'll miss it."

Rob opened the door for her, and ushered her out of the office and down the hallway. An uncomfortable silence loomed between them as Micah rummaged through her purse in search of change while walking toward the exit.

"Do you ride the bus often?" he asked.

"Only when I'm having car trouble," she replied and paused, looking up at his serious expression. "So I guess the answer is yes."

"If you're too late for your bus, I could call a taxi—"

"No, thank you," she said quickly, a little too quickly. Micah did not have money for cab fare, and she was not going to let this irritating young attorney offer to pay.

"It's too bad Mrs. Winslow isn't here. Perhaps she would have offered you a ride home," he suggested with the mischievous slant of his mouth brightening his otherwise dark features.

"I'd rather walk," Micah responded. The tone she had intended to be sharp somehow softened as she stared into his eyes.

"Yes, I suspect you would," Rob remarked with a quiet laugh. "I'll be leaving soon. If you'd care to take a chance on my driving, Spring Blossom Avenue is not far out of my way."

Spring Blossom Avenue. Her street. "How—"

"It's in your file," he answered. "I dictated the letter to 'Michael.' Remember?"

"Thanks, anyway, but I can catch the bus." She

started to leave. Part of her wanted to rush away from this situation, but her feet seemed firmly planted in the doorway, reluctant to move. "I'm sorry I couldn't help with your case."

Rob shrugged as if it was of no consequence. "You were honest," he commented as that smile slowly faded. "I have a feeling that's all you ever could be."

Honest. That's all she dared to be. The past had been difficult enough to put to rest. Micah had no plans to complicate her future. She stepped through the exit, letting the door fall shut behind her, and hurried away from the suite of offices and the young attorney she would not soon forget.

"Well? What did you think?" Carole asked the moment Micah opened the front door of her apartment to let her best friend enter. "Did you talk to him?"

"Yes. He's nice enough. Come to the kitchen, and I'll get you some lemonade."

"And good-looking? Didn't you think he was adorable?"

"Adorable, no. But he has a nice smile." Too nice, Micah thought.

"Come on, Micah. Lighten up! Rob Granston is the man for you, and I've known it since the day I met him. He did such a great job of handling the purchase of my tanning and hair salon—"

"I know, I know," Micah stated with a laugh. "I think you've mentioned that a time or two."

"And he's handsome and intelligent and funny and successful—"

"Okay, what is this? A commercial?"

"He's nearly perfect, Micah. I'd be interested in him myself if I didn't think of you every time I saw him. I'd feel like I was trying to take something away from you," Carole explained. "And think of what a strange chain of events has brought you two together! Maybe this is God's plan for your life. Isn't that what you're always looking for?"

"Really, Carole," Micah began as she pulled a pitcher from the refrigerator. "I think I can figure out God's plan for me, and I don't think it will be revealed through car accidents and appointments with attorneys. Be serious."

"I am. I mean, who would have thought that 'Old Yeller' would finally crash into some poor, unsuspecting soul, and you're the only witness!"

"I really wasn't a witness," she said as she retrieved two glasses from the cupboard. "I saw very little. I told Mrs. Winslow that very thing the night of the accident when she asked for my name and address, and I told the same thing to Mr. Granston this afternoon." She dropped several ice cubes into each glass.

"*Mr.* Granston? Come on, Micah. His name is Rob."

"And her name is Mrs. Winslow, not Old Yeller." Micah reminded her friend as she handed her a glass of lemonade.

"Don't get self-righteous on me. You've called

her Old Yeller plenty of times yourself when you've seen her coming."

"That was before I found out her name and before she ended up in the hospital with an injured back. She's no longer just the terrible driver of that big yellow car. She's a real person with real aches and pains and real problems—"

"And a *real* cute lawyer," Carole added before taking a sip of her drink.

Micah sat down at the kitchen table and tasted the lemonade she had poured for herself. "Anyway, I told Mr. Granston—"

"Rob. His name is Rob."

"We didn't get that friendly," Micah insisted. "You're the one who's dated him."

"A very casual luncheon date. Nothing to be jealous of."

"Jealous!" Micah exclaimed. "I'm not—"

"Listen, I've gotta go," Carole interrupted. "I've gotta be back at the shop for a seven-o'clock shampoo and set." She grabbed her purse and headed for the door. "Thanks for the lemonade. I'm sorry you and Rob didn't get off to a better start."

"There's nothing to start, Carole. I made an appointment like the letter requested, I answered his questions and left his office. End of story."

"That's what *you* think," Carole responded emphatically as she waved a quick goodbye before adding, "if I have my way, this is only the beginning."

Chapter Two

"Meet me there at noon."

"Carole, I have a ton of work to do. Are you sure we can be in and out of that place in an hour?" Micah held the telephone receiver between her shoulder and ear, wiping flour-covered hands on a dishcloth as she spoke to her friend.

"Positive," came Carole's quick response. "It's a good restaurant. Great food, fast service."

"Okay," Micah answered. Baking needed to be done and her neglected painting stared at her from the corner of the workshop, but she was getting hungry. "We'll need to hurry."

"No problem. Everyone in there will probably be in a hurry. Lots of business and professional people from downtown eat their lunches there. Lots of them."

"You're late," Carole observed aloud as Micah rushed into the crowded restaurant lobby over an hour later.

"I know, I know." Micah adjusted her skirt and blouse quickly. "I had to wait for the pies to come out of the oven."

"Pies?"

"Shepherd?" The hostess summoned them. "Party of two?"

"Yes," they replied simultaneously.

"You gave my name?" Micah asked.

"I always do when I make reservations for us. Shepherd is easier to spell than Zabotrowski."

They followed the hostess, weaving their way around tables, small and large, toward a booth along the wall. They slid into their seats and each received a menu.

"Would you like something from the bar?" the hostess inquired.

"No, I don't drink," Micah answered.

Carole shook her head. She did not care for anything, either.

They were assured their waitress would be along in a moment to take their orders and were left to review the menu.

"All you need to say is, 'No thanks,' Micah. You don't need to tell every hostess in central Ohio that you don't drink," Carole muttered. "Surely God doesn't expect that from you. I mean, it's not even one of the Ten Commandments. Now, tell me, why were you baking pies?''

''For the school bake sale tomorrow. The kids are trying to raise money for a trip to Washington, D.C.''

''Everyone? The whole school?''

''Just the fourth and fifth grades will be going. That is, if they can raise the money.'' Micah closed the menu. ''I think I'll have a salad and a bowl of vegetable soup.''

''Well, I'm starving so I'm going to have the turkey-bacon club, a side salad and...what kind of pies did you bake?''

''Apple, but they're for the school,'' Micah reminded her friend.

''Then I suppose I'll order some dessert.''

''Unless you want to buy one for a donation. Of course, I don't know how good they'll be. I haven't baked since last year—''

''Christmas, maybe? Remember? You baked two pumpkin pies at the cabin that weekend?''

''Oh, those.'' Micah covered her face with a hand. ''Don't remind me.''

''They weren't that bad. We ate them.''

''We had to. It was either that or no dessert,'' Micah recalled.

''Well, they might have been better if you had used the frozen crusts like I suggested.'' Carole placed her menu on the table.

''I really wanted to bake my own pies, Carole.

Taking something out of the freezer and putting it into the oven, it just doesn't seem right calling it your own.''

"Why not? I do it every evening. Out of the freezer and into the microwave. Beef Stroganoff, chipped beef, chicken à la king..."

"That's different."

"So how much for a pie? I mean, even if it's not great, at least it's a pie. There won't be anything that vaguely resembles one of those coming out of my oven in the foreseeable future. How much do you want?"

"Six dollars?" Micah asked more than stated.

"Sold," was Carole's reply as the waitress approached the booth.

With their orders placed, Micah glanced at her thin gold wristwatch. Grateful it was Friday and she had no teaching assignment today, Micah planned to spend the afternoon working on the painting she had started months ago: a little church in the country. Her long, slender fingers tucked a stray wisp of auburn hair behind her ear.

"Do you think 'living right' has anything to do with having great hair?" Carole asked, her words slicing into Micah's thoughts.

"What are you talking about?"

"You have the natural curls I've always wanted. Is it a gift from God for being good or something like that?"

"If I thought it would get you into church on Sunday, I'd be tempted to say 'yes.'"

"And tell a lie?" Carole quipped. "Surely not."

Several people walked past their booth, but Micah paid little attention to them. She had just picked up a bread stick from the basket on the table when she heard Carole's greeting.

"Hello, Rob! What a pleasant surprise!"

Rob. Micah quickly placed the bread stick on a saucer and picked up her napkin to wipe her fingers.

"Carole? It's been a long time since I've seen you," the distinctly male voice responded.

"Yes, it has. You know Micah Shepherd, don't you?" Carole's words bubbled with enthusiasm as she motioned toward Micah.

"Yes," he replied, the slightest hint of a smile tugging at one corner of his mouth. She noticed Rob's eyebrows lift as his gaze met and held hers. "We've met. How are you, Miss Shepherd?"

Micah smiled in response. "Fine, thank you." In some unexplainable way, she was both pleased and not pleased to see him again. So why was her heart pounding so loudly in her ears?

"I didn't realize that you and Miss Shepherd were friends." He spoke to Miss Zabotrowski, but his eyes remained firmly fixed upon her auburn-haired companion.

"Would you care to join us?" Carole offered.

Rob glanced at a nearby table. "Thank you, but

I'm meeting someone for lunch, and I'm running late, as it is.''

Micah exhaled a quiet sigh of relief before asking, "How is Mrs. Winslow?"

"About the same." Rob's piercing blue gaze burned through her as though silently questioning the motive for her inquiry and forcing Micah to look away. "It was nice to see you again, Carole, and you, too, Miss Shepherd."

Miss Shepherd. His formality irritated her, exactly the way he'd meant it to. Micah watched him turn and walk away, but not too far. He sat down at a table close by with an attractive brunette. Micah crunched into the bread stick.

"What's with you two? Just because you're not a good witness for Old Yeller doesn't mean you and Rob can't be friendly," Carole snapped.

"We're not friends," Micah replied, staring into the bowl of soup that the waitress set before her. "Mr. Granston is an attorney, I was a witness—a poor one—and that is the sum of our relationship."

Carole poured extra dressing over her salad. "Are you kidding? Did you see the way he looked at you? He couldn't take his eyes off you."

"Don't be ridiculous."

"It's true." Carole lowered her voice to a healthy whisper. "It was absolutely intense."

"Eat your salad and mind your own business, Carole," Micah warned softly before taking a drink from her water glass. He had looked surprised to see her again. Surprised, that was all. Wasn't it? She glanced toward the nearby table. The brunette was involved in some animated conversation, and Rob was being appropriately attentive.

"I'm just glad he's here today, even if he is with that dark-haired beauty. When I made the reservations, I was afraid I might have been wasting my time."

"This was intentional?" Micah placed her spoon on the table. "You assumed Rob would be here?"

"Rob?" Carole smiled. "I thought it was Mr. Granston?"

"Don't change the subject. You did this on purpose." Suddenly the meal didn't seem quite so inviting. "What if he knows why we're here?"

"Now you're the one who's being ridiculous. He's a lawyer, Micah, not a psychic. How could he possibly know my reason for inviting you here?"

Carole was right. He really couldn't know, Micah reasoned. "Is this where you had lunch with him?"

"Yes, but it was a business luncheon. I've told you that—"

"I'd really like to go home, Carole. My appetite seems to have disappeared."

"Leave without eating? What would he think if he saw us running out of here without having our lunch?"

Micah hesitated. "All right, you win. Let's eat and then go right away."

They gradually worked their way through their

meals, Carole a little more happily than Micah because Micah had trouble keeping her eyes from straying to the table that Rob and the brunette occupied. The last time she glanced up, the woman had disappeared—to the ladies' room, Micah supposed—and Rob's eyes rested directly on her. She smiled, a feeble little smile, in response, and looked back into her half-empty salad plate. The sooner she could get out of here, the better.

"I'm finished," Carole finally announced as she placed her napkin on the table, pulled her wallet from her purse and summoned their waitress to the table. "We'd like our checks now, please."

"They have already been taken care of, miss," the waitress stated.

"But we haven't seen them yet," Micah interjected.

Carole added, "There must be some mistake."

"There's no mistake. The gentleman you spoke with earlier paid the bills."

They both turned, but Rob was gone.

"Well, well, well," Carole mused aloud as they walked out of the dimly lit restaurant into the sunshine, warm and bright. "So that's the sum of your relationship."

"He obviously bought lunch for you," Micah insisted while walking toward Carole's car. "You know him and—"

"And I think he was buying for the pretty redhead seated at my table." Carole pulled open her car door, laughing. "If he caught a glimpse of your car on the way into the restaurant, he probably took pity on you, assuming that you couldn't afford to eat in a place this nice."

Micah shielded her eyes from the glare of the sun with one hand. "There's nothing wrong with my old station wagon," Micah replied, though she knew only too well that there was plenty wrong with it.

"No, nothing other than the fact that it's old and it's a station wagon." Carole glanced around the parking lot. "Where did you leave it?"

"I had trouble trying to start it," Micah admitted, "and I decided to walk. So Rob couldn't see my car even if he wanted to. Obviously, the lunch was for you."

"Do you want a ride home, or do you prefer standing in this hot sun arguing?"

The air felt sticky, and Micah was anxious to get home. The ride sounded good.

"I have a pie to pick up, remember?" Carole added.

The bake sale and the entire weekend flew by in a blur. So much so that Micah barely thought of her encounter with Rob Granston. Except for once or twice, late at night, just before she fell asleep. Deciding against calling to thank him for lunch, she left that task to Carole. After all, he was Carole's friend. Calling would seem presumptuous, as if she was assuming he'd picked up the check with her in mind when, certainly, that had not been the case, she reminded herself.

Micah ran a brush slowly through her long curls and applied a touch of peach lipstick to finish her morning routine. Another rainy Monday. What an unpredictable spring, rainy sometimes, hot and humid others. But today Micah returned to a familiar school, and that brightened her spirits regardless of the weather. When two years of substitute teaching wore thin, she had gladly agreed to finish out the school year at Wellspring Elementary as a replacement for a teacher on maternity leave. It surprised Micah to discover how much she enjoyed greeting the same young faces each day. Maybe she would consider looking for a full-time position soon. Maybe something permanent was what she needed in her life. She had already lived here for two years, longer than she had stayed in any other city since her eighteenth birthday. Columbus suited her, especially the German Village location of her apartment with its brick-lined streets and quaint buildings, and as long as the thought of leaving saddened her, she stayed.

Meow...meow.... Micah laughed lightly as she hurried toward the door and the pitiful noise.

"Poor baby." She opened the door a few inches, enough to allow a multicolored cat to enter. "Mrs. Poe puts you outside every morning, rain or shine, doesn't she, Patches? How about some milk?"

Micah poured the liquid into a saucer, and then

set it on the kitchen floor. Stroking the cat's damp fur, she heard that familiar purring begin. "There you go, babe. That should make you a little happier, but you're going to get fat having two breakfasts every morning. I know Mrs. Poe feeds you well."

The morning paper cluttered the table where Micah had been reading it and eating toast, but one glance at the clock told her that the mess would have to wait to be straightened up until evening.

"Hurry, Patches." Gathering her umbrella and books, Micah started for the door with her landlady's cat scurrying after her. It paused to rub against Micah's ankles and nearly knocked her down in the process. "Out the door, Patches." She gave the cat a gentle shove with her foot, forcing the feline into the steady spring shower. "Sorry to rush you, but I've got to go," she said and turned the key in the lock, twisting the knob to be certain it had locked securely.

"See you later, kitty." Unexpected sadness rained down on her as surely as the light drops. She was twenty-eight years old, and all she had to come home to every evening was Patches...a cat that didn't even belong to her. Surely there must be something, someone more for her out there. Why didn't the Lord show her His plan for her life? she wondered again as she had done many times. She already knew what she *couldn't* do, but the whole city wasn't filled with attorneys, was it? Why couldn't she meet a pastor, a math teacher or a truck driver...?

Micah stacked her books on the front seat. Or why couldn't she be happy alone? She had been content with her life until recently. When had that changed? She leaned into the car, her eyes coming to rest on a painting placed there earlier. The little country church with a backdrop of a summer-blue sky—the same gentle blue of Rob Granston's eyes.

Suddenly, she knew when the contentment had vanished.

Chapter Three

~~~~~

"This job fair is a wonderful idea, Angela," Micah said to the young, dark-haired woman who taught in the next classroom.

"It's an annual event. I know the kids are rather young to absorb much about the different careers, but it's never too early for them to start considering the possibilities for their future."

They walked toward the gymnasium. The children had been ushered into the gym immediately following their lunch period to view the Career Day displays set up there. Posters, pamphlets, booths with displays and even a miniature firehouse filled the area. Several firefighters, military personnel, a chef with baked goods to sample, a secretary with modern business equipment to demonstrate, a nurse and an airplane pilot were present, along with a martial arts expert who was practicing on mats in the middle of the floor. Numerous other occupations were represented, as well.

"I have three children," Angela stated as they entered the crowded gym. "And they all, as young as they are, know what they want to be when they grow up. Nathan, my ten-year-old wants to be a doctor, David, my middle child, loves airplanes, so he's going to be a pilot, and Heather, well, she wants to be a teacher like her mommy."

Micah was about to ask Angela a few questions about her children, when she noticed him. At school. In the gym. Smiling and walking toward her. She could hardly believe her eyes. But after reaching her, he leaned over and kissed the other teacher on the cheek.

"Hi, Rob. Thanks for coming," Angela greeted him.

Micah stood speechless. How many times would she encounter this man? And what was he doing kissing Angela?

"Glad to help out, little sister," Rob said as he studied Micah's confused expression. "So we meet again, Miss Shepherd."

"Yes...I..." She remained at a loss for words, and he was looking at her as if it didn't matter.

"I am the official representative of the legal profession today. My sister couldn't con a judge into coming, so she settled for me."

"Now don't tell lies, Robert. You know you were my first choice," Angela commented as the three of them started walking through the tables and displays. "I'm surprised you and Micah know each other."

"Yes, it seems rather strange to keep running into each other. Are you sure you haven't been following me, Miss Shepherd?"

"I could accuse you of exactly the same thing, Mr. Granston," Micah quickly remarked.

"Perhaps, rightfully so," he answered quietly, his disturbing gaze never wavering.

"So, tell me, Robert. How do you plan to compete with martial arts demonstrations and samples of the chef's cooking?" Angela inquired.

"Speaking of cooking," Micah interrupted, "thank you for buying lunch the other day. It was very kind of you."

"You're welcome," he replied and then turned his attention to his sister's question. "I've set up a courtroom." They moved to Rob's area of the floor and viewed what appeared to be a mock trial in progress. "We've selected twelve impartial jurors, after explaining the words *impartial* and *juror* to them. And we have a judge, a prosecutor and a defense attorney. I put everything on hold until I could find you. I thought you'd like this."

Angela was beaming. Obviously she did like it very much.

"What's the judge's name?" Rob asked the small, blond boy in the judge's seat.

"Sam Oleson."

"The Honorable Sam Oleson presiding over this trial," Rob announced. "And, ladies, we need an alleged criminal. Would either of you care to do the honors?"

Rob looked only at Micah as he spoke, and Angela laughed at the lack of attention. "I guess you're it, Micah."

"No, thanks," she replied, stepping back. "I have some other exhibits to attend to. I don't have time to be tried and convicted."

The children responded enthusiastically. "C'mon, Miss Shepherd. Be the bad guy!"

"The 'alleged' bad guy," Rob clarified as he reached for Micah's hand.

"No," she stated quickly as she moved away from Rob and the "judge's" bench. "Angela will make a better bad guy for you."

"Thanks a lot!" came Angela's response. "What a compliment."

"We want Miss Shepherd! We want Miss Shepherd!" the children chanted.

"Hold it down, guys," Rob said as he raised his hand to quiet down his group. "Miss Shepherd looks a little too honest to play a criminal."

"I'll do it," Angela intervened, apparently sensing Micah's nervousness. "I just hope I don't become a victim of type-casting."

"Guilty! Guilty!" cried the young participants.

"What kind of jury are you?" Rob asked before laughing at the children's reaction to his sister.

Micah edged away from the scene, hoping to slip out unnoticed. Rob organized the children into the arrangement he wanted, but not without glancing up curiously at Micah as she walked from the circle of activity.

Micah rubbed her arms briskly as she fought the invading chill. Years had passed since she had been part of a courtroom setting. Time changes things, or so she had heard; but she was under the growing conviction that time did not change anything but pages on the calendar.

There were colorful displays and some rather plain exhibits, but they all received adequate attention from curious children in no hurry to get back to the classroom.

The martial arts expert drew the largest gathering of children. Oohs and aahs filled that portion of the gymnasium as the youngsters freely expressed how impressed they were with the performances. Micah watched for a few minutes, wondering how martial arts qualified for a Career Day exhibit. Not exactly a nine-to-five job, she considered. But then, neither was painting. She stopped at the small concession stand and bought a soda.

The elderly lady who had come for her family-owned bakery was a major attraction, and it only took a taste of one of the woman's hundreds of thumbprint cookies filled with strawberry jam to understand her popularity. But Micah ate a second, just to confirm her theory.

The afternoon slipped away, and soon the children were herded back to their classrooms by Angela, Micah and the other teachers for school dismissal. The bell soon rang and the children were "free." At least that was the impression they gave as they burst from the confines of the long brick building and filled the sidewalks with skipping feet, endless chatter and an occasional word of profanity.

"Children," Micah said quietly to herself. So few of them were the sweet, innocent kids they deserved to be at their tender ages. Many knew far more of the world's harsh ways and heartaches than their teachers, who had grown up in gentler decades. Micah closed the classroom window with a thud.

"Micah?" Angela stuck her head around the corner of the doorway, peering into the classroom. "Everyone is in a hurry to get out of here this afternoon. Are you ready?"

"Almost." Micah rearranged a few books and flipped off the light switch. "What's the rush?"

"We all have to be back here at seven o'clock for a special meeting regarding funding cuts." Angela's smile seemed a bit mischievous as she offered, "You're invited to attend."

"No, thanks. Not attending that kind of meeting is one of the fringe benefits of being a sub." She exited the classroom and walked down the hallway with Angela. "The gym is a mess. Will it be straightened out in time for your meeting?"

"Didn't I tell you? The meeting will be held in

the cafeteria. They're leaving the displays in the gym until tomorrow afternoon. Career Day was such a success with the kids that the principal arranged for most of the volunteers to return tomorrow for a couple of hours.'' They neared the front door.

''Rob is one of the only ones who can't come back,'' Angela explained, disappointment obvious in her tone. ''He has a hearing first thing in the morning.''

''That's too bad,'' Micah said. ''For the kids, I mean.''

''Uh-huh,'' Angela said in agreement. ''I didn't know that you and Rob knew each other. He's never mentioned you.''

''We met because of a car accident,'' Micah told her. ''He represents the injured driver, and I was supposedly a witness, but I didn't really see much.'' Abruptly, Micah changed the subject. ''So Career Day was quite a hit with the kids.''

''Too much so,'' was Angela's sharp reply. ''Remember, I told you that my son Nathan wanted to be a doctor?''

''Want*ed*? Past tense?'' Micah responded.

''He's giving up medicine for a career in karate.'' Micah laughed.

''This had better be just a phase he's going through,'' Angela said. ''I'm going to have his father discuss potential gross income with him tonight.''

Micah laughed heartily. ''He's only ten years old,

Angela. Give him time. How much could he understand about potential gross income anyway?"

"He'll know plenty about it by bedtime this evening. His future wife, wherever the poor child may be, should be out there somewhere praying that I can talk some sense into him." Angela pushed open the door.

"See you tomorrow. Good luck with Nathan."

"Thanks," Angela responded as she left Micah standing in the doorway.

"You'll have to let your kids choose their own careers, Angela."

"Not when they're eight and ten, I don't," She waved as she neared her car. "Well, the kids are waiting for me, and I have a lot of 'steering in the right direction' to do tonight...and for the next decade or so. See you!"

Micah pulled the door shut tightly, remaining in the building. Turning to her right, she walked down the hallway toward the gym and the side exit that led to the parking lot where she had parked her car. The building had cleared out quickly, and she hastened her pace a little as she continued down the long, empty corridor. Then she heard the comforting sounds of someone else in the building. Probably a janitor, she assumed. They worked later than everyone else normally did so they could lock up the school. Metal chairs that were being folded and returned to their rack made clanking, banging noises that reverberated through the gymnasium. She walked past the bakery display and the unattended office equipment of the secretarial exhibit toward the noise and the side door leading to the parking lot.

"Hello, again."

Micah gasped at the unexpected voice.

"I didn't mean to frighten you," Rob said as he folded the last chair.

Micah's hand was on her chest, feeling the rapid pounding of her heart. "What are you doing here? I thought everyone but the janitor had gone."

Rob motioned toward the vacant floor space where his mock courtroom drama had played out. "I'm putting away the chairs and tables that I used today since I can't come back tomorrow."

"Angela said you had a hearing in the morning." She pushed her hair away from her face and adjusted the books that were shifting in her arms. "The kids really liked your presentation."

Rob smiled, a lazy kind of smile. Micah noticed her heart continued to pound too quickly. And she was no longer frightened.

"Some of them seemed to get caught up in it. I think Wellspring Elementary School has several potential attorneys in it."

He stopped talking, and Micah knew she should respond, but she had barely heard his comment, having been too busy studying the contrast between his black hair and blue eyes. The soft pastel of his pale blue shirt seemed to enhance the clear color of his gaze. After all, Micah reasoned, artists notice things like that. Don't they?

"You don't care much for courtroom drama, do you?" Rob asked.

"No," she replied flatly. "I don't."

He was no longer smiling as he considered her serious expression, and he did not respond. Micah suspected he was waiting for her to elaborate, and since she had no intention of doing that, she repeated what she'd said earlier.

"You had a nice presentation, and the kids really did enjoy it. It's a shame you can't come back tomorrow and give more of them a chance to be part of the trial."

"Maybe next year we'll try again," he replied. "Maybe by then I can convince you to participate."

"Hello," came a voice from the other side of the military display. An elderly janitor stepped away from the booth out into full view. "How did Career Day go?"

"Very well," Micah answered. "It's to be continued tomorrow, so at least you don't have to tear down the displays tonight."

"It's a good thing, too, 'cause I don't feel like doing much of anything." He wiped beads of perspiration from his forehead with a handkerchief. "Too much lunch, I guess. Feels like a bad case of indigestion."

"Let's get a seat for you," Rob was saying as he reached for a folding chair. "You look pale."

"Are you okay?" Micah extended a hand to grab the man's arm as he wobbled and then slumped to the floor.

"Are you all right? Can you hear me?" Micah knelt down, frantically shaking the man's shoulder.

Working quickly, Rob loosened the janitor's shirt and tilted the head back. He leaned near, watching the chest area that failed to rise and fall. Pressing his fingers against the man's neck, he searched for a heartbeat. "No pulse, no breathing," he said. "Get his arm out of the way," he ordered, and Micah complied. "He needs to be lying flat."

Micah's own heart raced wildly. Did people really die like this? In gymnasiums on warm Monday afternoons?

"Find a phone, Micah. Call for help," he instructed then began the required breaths before starting compressions. Micah had taken CPR classes, too, but that had been six months ago. Maybe longer.

"Now, Micah, call," Rob demanded. "One and two and three and..."

Micah heard Rob count as she ran across the gym toward a phone that she thought she remembered seeing in the kitchen. Grabbing the receiver, she dialed 911. The operator answered after the first ring. Confirm the location? There had been so many different schools she had subbed in this year. "Oh, Lord, help me remember...Wellspring Elementary School! Yes, that's it. It's on the corner of Oak and...something...I'm not sure...yes...it's a heart attack, we think...right, no pulse, no breathing... yes, CPR... Please hurry!'' she added before ending the conversation. Running back to the south side of the huge gymnasium, her footsteps echoed off the walls in hollow sounds.

"Five minutes," she said as she knelt beside Rob. "The emergency squad is on its way."

After the next series of compressions, Rob stopped to check the janitor's pulse. "Still nothing."

"I can help. I think I remember the two-man compressions," Micah offered.

Rob nodded, and Micah leaned forward to give the next series of breaths. Less than five minutes later, help arrived. The counting and compressions continued until Rob and Micah were relieved by the rescue team and a pulse was reestablished.

Everyone acted promptly and precisely, and it took only a brief time to transport the man into the waiting emergency vehicle. Soon the squad pulled away, lights flashing, sirens blaring.

"We did it," Micah said softly in near disbelief as tears filled her eyes. They stood, alone, on the steps outside the school building.

"Don't cry, Micah," Rob offered as he placed an arm around her shoulders. "We did it. He's still alive."

"Yes." She wiped her eyes with the back of her hand. "I can't believe I actually remembered what I was supposed to do, and did it!"

Rob smiled. "That's what the training is all about."

"And you...you seemed so calm."

Rob shook his head. "No, I'm just a good actor. I was as scared as you were."

They turned and Rob moved his arm away from her as they walked into the gym.

"Have you used CPR before?" Micah inquired.

"No, but the senior partner at the law firm I'm with has a heart problem. He requires all staff members to participate in CPR classes every year. I think he's afraid of dying," Rob commented with a wry smile while bending over to help pick up the papers and books Micah had dropped when the crisis began. "Some people are, you know." He looked over at her. "You really did a good job today."

"Thank you. I think I'll call the hospital tonight to find out how he's doing."

After all of her belongings had been retrieved, they walked out the side door and entered the gravel parking lot. A sudden gust of wind caught Micah's hair and blew it around her face. "The station wagon is mine." She pointed to her car while pushing back her hair.

He walked her to the old, well-worn wagon and opened the door for her. "May I ask you a personal question?"

Micah climbed into the driver's seat and looked up at him. "We just saved a man's life together. I

guess that entitles you to one personal question.''
She smiled.

"You have no husband or children…right?"

"Right."

"So what does a young, pretty woman like yourself need with a vehicle that seats ten people?"

Micah turned around and pulled back a sheet that
covered some of her art supplies. "People aren't
what I'm transporting. I need room to haul these
supplies and my paintings back and forth to the different art classes I teach and to the festivals where
I work in the summer and fall."

"Festivals? You travel around to festivals?"

"Yes," she answered, and she draped the sheet
back over her frames and other paraphernalia.
"Windmill Days, Fourth of July carnivals, Scare-
crow Festival…I've sold quite a few paintings that
way, and I make some extra money on caricatures."

"You're an interesting woman, Micah Shepherd," Rob commented as he closed the car door
for her.

"Thank you…I think," she replied as she picked
up her sunglasses from the dashboard and pushed a
handful of auburn curls over her shoulder. He was
interesting, too. Good manners, thoughtful, caring…

"Could I convince you to have dinner with me?"
he asked.

His words might or might not, but those blue eyes
definitely could. Sliding her sunglasses into place,

the effect of his gaze was not quite as shattering. "I still think Mrs. Winslow drives likes a maniac."

He smiled. "You're entitled to your opinion. Seven o'clock?"

Seven o'clock. After all, Micah reasoned, he had agreed to come to the job fair because his sister needed him there. He seemed harmless enough. What kind of man was this she was nearly ready to refuse? For heaven's sake, the guy even knew CPR.

"What do you like? Seafood? Steak? Chinese?" he asked.

"Pancakes," she answered. They could have dinner. Just dinner.

"Pancakes?" Rob repeated with a frown darkening his expression. "That's what you want?"

"That's what I was going to have at home tonight. Pancakes and orange juice. I already owe you a meal for lunch at the restaurant. So will you join me tonight for pancakes?"

"Sounds good," Rob responded.

"Seven o'clock?" she said.

"I'll see you then." He waved, and then turned to walk away.

"You'll need my address," she called after him.

"It's 793 Spring Blossom Avenue. The Winslow file. I have a good memory," he replied.

Micah drove from the lot and watched his medium-size maroon car follow her a few blocks or so until he turned off on a path of his own. Micah thought briefly of the symbolism. Ultimately, they would go their separate ways. They had to; the choice was not theirs to make. But one dinner with her could not hurt his career or break her heart. Could it?

Micah turned onto a brick street leading through the Village and drove past the numerous shops, restaurants and offices that lined the familiar route to her apartment. Usually she enjoyed looking at the well-kept homes and remodeled brick buildings, but tonight her mind was on her nearly empty refrigerator and cluttered apartment. She hoped he really did like pancakes and orange juice because, except for a possible package of sausages and a bowl of tossed salad, pancake ingredients were virtually all she had on hand.

Her large station wagon took up enough space for two smaller cars, she thought as she pulled up to the curb. She shut off the engine and moved her parking permit from the dashboard to its place on the rearview mirror. Then she hurried from the car, through the iron gate and into her small but immaculate courtyard.

Her apartment was in the rear of the complex and quite secluded. Micah appreciated the privacy and quiet when she worked on her paintings. Sliding the key into the lock, she pushed open the door, hoping she hadn't left too big of a mess that morning. Reaching into the straw basket mounted just outside the doorway, she pulled several items of mail from the wicker container.

"Good evening, Patches," she said to the cat who ran down the sidewalk to greet her. The pet rubbed around her ankles and had to be held back to be kept from entering the apartment.

A sigh of relief escaped her as she saw that the place was fairly neat. She placed the mail and her books on the end table beside her small floral-print sofa in the living room then went to the kitchen to gather up sections of the morning newspaper strewn over the table. Grabbing the coffee cup and saucer left from breakfast, she plunked them into the dishpan, and after checking the refrigerator for the items she needed and finding a package of sausage that she had hoped was there, she headed for the bathroom to shower and change. Then, right on time, the doorbell rang.

"Hello, again," Rob said as she opened the door.

"Hi. Tulips?" she commented, admiring the bouquet he handed to her. "Thank you. They're beautiful, Rob, but a pancake dinner hardly justifies flowers."

"We worked well together this afternoon, Micah. We have reason to celebrate. I hope I selected a kind you are not allergic to." He paused. "You look beautiful."

"Thank you." Her soft casual dress had swirls of pastel colors making up its design. She knew it was lovely. That's why she wore it, even after a ten-minute argument with herself about her choice. "The flowers are perfect. Please, come in."

Rob stepped into the living room. "Your apartment wasn't easy to find, tucked away in this little courtyard."

"It is secluded. That's one of the reasons I like it."

"I checked with the hospital," Rob said as she closed the front door. "The janitor is doing better. He's in ICU, and his name is Donald Lacey."

"And he's still alive. That's wonderful!" Micah exclaimed, so excited by the report that she nearly hugged Rob. But she caught herself in time and kept her feet firmly planted where they were. Suddenly, she felt awkward, standing there with him. "I'll start the pancakes. The sausage is nearly ready."

"Is there anything I can do to help?"

"No, thanks. The table is set, and the batter is made. Just make yourself comfortable." Micah motioned toward the sofa, offering him a seat. Then she disappeared into the kitchen. Pulling a large white vase from the cabinet below the sink, she filled it with water and the fresh-cut flowers and set it on the table.

Micah listened to the sound of several books being pulled from her oak bookcase and then, after a moment, being returned one by one.

"You have a nice apartment."

She looked up at the nearness of his voice. Rob stood in the doorway of the kitchen, watching her pour pancake batter onto the hot griddle.

"Thanks. It's small but I like it." She pulled a spatula from the silverware drawer.

"Yellow must be your favorite color," he commented as he glanced around the narrow white room accented with yellow curtains, yellow canisters and various other brightly colored kitchen accessories, including the yellow flowers she had stenciled across the top of the walls.

"Favorite color in general, but not a favorite in clothing." She turned the pancakes. "All this red hair and yellow just don't mix."

"I've yet to see a color that you wouldn't look lovely in," Rob stated.

Micah's green eyes widened in surprise at his statement. She looked over at him, meeting his steady gaze. "Thank you," she offered quietly.

"No need to thank me," he replied. "It's just a statement of fact."

Micah returned her gaze to the browning sausage rather than look into his eyes. No one had ever said anything like that to her. At least, no one over the age of eight.

"I'll bet you've broken the hearts of quite a few little guys in your classes."

Micah glanced up, and smiled. "One or two, I'm afraid." She turned down the burner under the meat. "It seems easy for them to develop a crush on a substitute teacher."

"I can understand that," he commented.

Micah continued, "Anyway, it can sometimes be

awkward." Just as awkward as this moment in her kitchen with Robert Granston. "I'm usually left wondering if I handled the situation well." When she stacked the first pile of pancakes onto a small plate, Micah accidently knocked the empty measuring cup from the counter and both she and Rob reached for it. But she was closer and quicker.

"I've got it," she said quietly as they leaned together momentarily. They were so close, Micah felt his breath flow across her cheek, and for an instant she wondered if he was about to kiss her. But he only touched the softness of her hair that swung freely around her shoulders. Then he stood up, moving away from her.

"Dinner is almost ready," Micah commented and returned to the job at hand.

Within a few minutes they sat down at the kitchen table. Then came the moment Micah knew would be difficult. It always was. Even after a decade of dealing with it. She bowed her head and offered a brief prayer, in front of this man she hardly knew. When finished, she looked up to meet his gaze and found nothing questioning or negative in his eyes. Only acceptance, and maybe approval, which was more than she expected. Micah smiled and passed the syrup, and they shared a late-evening breakfast.

"So, how long have you been a Christian?" Rob asked.

"Ten years. That obvious, huh?" she replied between sips of orange juice.

Rob smiled. "Well, you quietly prayed your way through Mr. Lacey's heart attack, and you audibly thanked God for our dinner, not knowing what my reaction would be. That's pretty strong evidence."

"And just what *is* your reaction?" Micah asked.

"One of respect," he responded as something cold—no, sad—flickered through the blue eyes that held her gaze too easily. His smile slowly faded.

"To give your life to God or not, it's a choice we all eventually make, Rob."

"I've tried it, Micah. It didn't work for me." Rob turned his attention to the coffee cup in his hand.

"What went wrong?"

He shook his head. "It would take less time to tell you what didn't go wrong." His smile returned. "And I don't want to spend this evening talking about something unpleasant that happened years ago."

So Micah left the subject alone, hoping... knowing that sometime they'd come back to it. In the meantime, Micah's school stories and Rob's tales of unusual cases kept conversation and laughter flowing freely throughout the meal.

"So when she asked me to come to the job fair, I couldn't refuse. I have a hard time saying no to my little sister," Rob said as Micah poured a third, or maybe it was the fourth, round of coffee. She had lost count.

"It must be nice," Micah said and took a sip from the cup she cradled in her hand.

"Having a sister to talk you into things?"

"Having a sister, period."

Rob looked at her silently for a moment. "You don't have any brothers or sisters?"

"No. My parents weren't young when they had me, so I am their only child."

"Then you must be very close to your parents," he commented.

"Dad and I were close for a long time." Her fingers moved instinctively to the heart locket that hung loosely around her neck today and most days, and Rob's eyes followed her movements. "But now..." she began, and then hesitated.

Rob studied her wary gaze and waited.

"...we're not," she concluded with a half-hearted smile.

Rob started to respond, but then apparently changed his mind and returned his attention to the piece of gold jewelry Micah touched so lovingly.

"That's a beautiful locket. I think you've worn it every time I've seen you," he remarked. "Was it a gift from him?"

"Yes, from years ago." She cleared her throat nervously and attempted to move on. "Being an only child wasn't so bad really. I had lots of friends around when I was very young. But if I ever have any children of my own—"

"'If' you have children? You're a teacher. You must love kids. I'd think you'd want a whole houseful," Rob remarked.

Micah stared at her empty plate. Now they were venturing into territory better left alone. Why did it have to happen so soon?

"I do enjoy children, but I don't know how I feel about a whole houseful of them." She stood up and began gathering up the dishes.

"I'll help you," he offered as he rose from his chair.

"There's no need."

"You did the cooking. The least I can do is wash the dishes."

"A compromise?" Micah smiled. "I'll wash, you dry."

"Fair enough."

Soon they stood side by side at the kitchen sink, working together for the second time in one day.

"I probably should tell you what happened with Mrs. Winslow and her maniacal driving," Rob offered as he placed a cup in the dish rack.

"Something good, I hope. Not another accident?"

"No more accidents," he stated. "She voluntarily gave up her driving privileges. You were only the first in a long line of people to express concern about Mrs. Winslow remaining behind the wheel of any vehicle. So, thanks for your honesty."

"You're welcome," she replied and handed him a clean plate. The conversation returned to brothers and sisters, and Rob didn't mind talking about his.

"That didn't take long," Micah remarked while rinsing the empty dishpan. Then she switched off the light and they exited the small kitchen, moving into the more comfortable, but not much larger, living room.

"I haven't eaten pancakes since I had breakfast with my sister and her kids a couple of Saturdays ago."

"I don't know Angela very well, but she's been very friendly to me."

"She's great even if she does talk me into job fairs," he conceded. "Is this your work?" Rob motioned toward a set of four small paintings hanging above the sofa. Each picture depicted the same covered bridge flanked on both sides by wooded areas, but each scene brought to life the heart of a different season. From windswept spring to the frigid blast of a winter snowstorm.

In answer to his question, she nodded.

"Micah, these are beautiful." Rob studied the pieces. "It looks to me like you should *teach* art. To adults, I mean."

Micah smiled. "I do. At the tech school some evenings."

"Could I see more?"

"If you like." Micah led him back through the kitchen to the rear door. Opening it, they entered a tiny workroom enclosed in glass. Micah switched on the light. "This is another reason I keep this apartment. It's my favorite room."

Rob glanced around the room, surveying the work on the canvases Micah had stored there. A ballerina in midair in soft pastels, a brightly colored hot-air balloon amid a shimmering blue sky, children laughing and playing on a merry-go-round, and several others including ocean and seashore scenes and some small, delicate works of flowers and birds. "These are wonderful..."

"Thank you." Micah caught her lower lip between her teeth, restricting her smile.

"The kids in the playground and the ballerina...they look like they could walk right out of the pictures...and the ocean...it seems...restless." He glanced at her with surprise evident in his eyes. "It all looks so real."

"Thank you," she said with a light laugh. "It's supposed to."

"But these are all finished," he commented. "What are you working on now?"

"An oil painting of an old white church that I discovered one day while I was driving through the country."

Rob scanned the contents of the room, and not seeing the piece she'd referred to, he glanced up in question.

"I ran out of room in here. The painting is in the back room. I'll show it to you when it's finished," Micah replied, instantly regreting the insinuation of a future for them. There could be none, and she thought she must be losing her mind even to consider it. She needed a change of subject, a change of mind.

"Do you go to church anywhere?" she asked.

"Not anymore," Rob answered. "I accepted Christ when I was thirteen, Micah. I was active with the youth group, all the kinds of things you'd expect. Everything seemed great until my best friend, Nick, died. Then...it didn't seem so real anymore. I stopped going."

"How did he die?" Micah asked hesitantly, not knowing if she should pursue this subject.

"Car accident on a rainy night." Rob checked the clock on the wall over Micah's easel. "It's nearly midnight. I had no idea it was that late."

Neither had Micah, and she looked toward the timepiece. Midnight. So that's when it ended. Now she knew how Cinderella must have felt. This had to end. Now. Because the more she knew of Rob, the more she wanted to know. The longer they talked, the longer she wanted to talk. And this man, standing in the middle of Micah's paintings, was a man she could love. Easily. Maybe eternally.

"We both have to get up early in the morning. I should be going."

Yes, Micah thought, you should. But she said nothing as she turned to walk with him to the front door. How could it be so late? Where had the evening gone? Micah swallowed hard, fighting back the words that threatened to flow from her.

They reached the entryway in silence, and when Micah reached for the doorknob, so did Rob. It could have been an awkward moment, but it was not. Rob's strong hand closed over Micah's as naturally as if he had planned it, his fingers linking through hers, warmth against warmth. Micah bit her lower lip gently as she stood facing Rob in the narrow entryway, wanting him to stay longer, wanting him to go. Dinner together. That's all it was supposed to be. Just pancakes and orange juice.

"Micah..." The tenderness with which he spoke her name calmed the rambling argument running through her head. "I want to see you again. You know that, don't you?"

She nodded, not trusting herself to speak. She knew. And if *she* knew, then *he* must know the attraction was mutual. And strong. And crazy.

"Rob, I don't think—"

"Dinner, tomorrow night?" he offered, overruling her objections. "I could pick you up around six-thirty?"

Dinner. It could never be just dinner again. Not with them. "No, I don't think..." What could she say? Micah had never been good at hiding her feelings and she respected honesty too much to really try. "Rob, it just wouldn't be a good idea."

"I'll take you out for pancakes if you like." He smiled. Just the way she knew he would.

"No." She smiled back. "I've reached my quota of maple syrup for the week."

"Then how about steak and a salad?" He squeezed, then released her hand and Micah wished he hadn't.

"Rob, you don't understand—"

"So, explain it to me." He stepped out into the courtyard. "Tomorrow. Six-thirty."

"It won't work. Let's not start—"

"We've already started, Micah. Let's see where it goes."

Down a dead-end street. That's where it would lead them. But with this man, Micah suspected, it would be an interesting journey.

"You're the one who will regret this," she offered quietly, truthfully.

"Tomorrow night. We'll discuss this reluctance of yours over a meal. Then we'll decide whether or not it's valid. Fair enough?"

"You're a hard man to argue with," Micah agreed with mixed emotions.

"I chose the right profession, didn't I?" Rob stated more than asked.

Micah cringed. Could he have possibly said anything worse?

Rob hesitated for a moment, standing just outside her door. "Thank you for tonight."

Micah smiled and nodded. He was welcome, and he knew it.

Then he offered only a quiet "Good night," and Micah watched him walk through the moonlit courtyard.

"You had dinner with him last night and you're going out again tonight?" Carole shrieked, and Micah held the telephone receiver away from her ear until Carole quieted down.

"Don't get too excited. We're going out to dinner and then we're going to discuss why we can't see each other anymore," Micah said as she stared into the mirror above the telephone and applied blush to her cheekbones. "I've got to finish getting ready, Carole. He'll be here by six-thirty and I'm not ready. Could I call you later?"

"You'll be too busy to call me." Carole giggled. "Forget that nonsense about not seeing him anymore. Hang on to this guy, Micah."

"Carole—"

"What is it with you and lawyers, anyway?"

Micah froze, makeup brush in her hand. "Why do you say that?"

"That's it, isn't it? There's no other reason not to be crazy about him," Carole responded sharply. "I know you don't like to talk about your past, but it's ridiculous to let Rob slip away because of something that happened years ago."

"Carole, if you—"

"So you've been hurt by someone. Big deal! Who hasn't?"

"That was a long time ago, and it's not the only reason."

"Was the other guy a lawyer, too? Do you not trust any attorneys?"

Micah remained silent for a few seconds, remembering. "He was a college student." Her voice softened as she spoke, and she studied her frowning expression in the mirror. "I really don't want to get into this."

"Maybe you need to talk about it. If not with me, with someone. I remember what happened when you dated Scott. Remember him?"

The government teacher. They dated for several weeks, until he was accepted to law school.

"The minute he started taking night classes, you stopped seeing him. And now Rob, how could you *not* like him...but you won't let it happen!"

Micah's grip tightened on the receiver. Saying goodbye to Scott had been easy, even after several weeks of dating. But Rob... She had spent only a few hours with him, and yet...

"*Nothing* is going to happen if you don't let me get ready for my date." Micah attempted to speak in a lighthearted manner.

"Okay, okay. I'll shut up, but *think* about what you're doing. Think about Rob. About the present, the future, not the past!"

"I'll call you later," Micah replied before replacing the receiver. And she wondered... Today... tomorrow... Could they be separated from yesterday?

Chapter Four

"I'm really not hungry enough for a steak," Micah commented as she reviewed the menu. "I think I'll have a salad with the sourdough bread."

"That's all?" Rob closed his menu.

"That's plenty," she replied. She wouldn't mention how much she had snacked during the afternoon.

"All right, Miss Shepherd." He studied her, looking at her that same way he had in his office the first time they met. As if he wanted to say something but wasn't certain it should be said.

"Have we taken a step backward in time that I'm not aware of and returned to the days of 'Miss Shepherd' and 'Mr. Granston'?"

"No, but you've barely said a word since I picked you up, and you're dressed rather businesslike," he answered from across the table, glancing at what was visible of the bittersweet-red suit and blouse of oyster white.

It had been a deliberate choice. Micah wanted to have a nice evening, but not too nice.

"You don't like what I'm wearing?" she asked, looking down at her clothes.

"Your outfit accomplishes its purpose," he stated with the firm line of his mouth curving into a smile.

"So you don't like it?"

"Oh, but I do," he responded. "It's very professional. If you're ever called upon to represent someone in court, I suggest you wear it."

Micah's eyes sparked at the sound of his stinging words.

"Then I think it would be appropriate for a meeting with an attorney."

"This is not a meeting with an attorney," he replied quietly. "This is a date...a date with a man who is very much interested in you." He looked away, toward the waiter who approached their table, before returning his gaze to her. "I'm wondering whether your distrust is of me personally or of all men in general."

"Would the lady care for something from the bar, Mr. Granston?" The question from the waiter sliced into their discussion.

"No," Rob answered without asking Micah. "Thank you, anyway, Henry."

The waiter nodded and left them alone again.

"How did you know that I don't drink? You didn't ask."

"You don't, do you?" Rob responded. "It wouldn't fit with your Christian view of things."

"That's true, but why didn't the waiter offer to bring something for you? You've given up your Christianity." Micah's words sounded harsher than she had meant them to.

"I'm in here a lot, and Henry knows I never order anything from the bar for myself," Rob explained. "I have a brother-in-law who's an alcoholic, and, well, it's not a pretty picture, Micah."

"Angela's husband?" she asked in disbelief.

"Yes," he answered and smiled. "It seems I couldn't save my little sister from all of life's heartaches."

"It was never your responsibility to do that in the first place," Micah commented.

"Spoken like an only child," he said quietly.

Rob's remark hurt more than Micah would admit. She slid her menu over to him, and he picked it up, putting it with his as their waiter approached to take their order.

"Why does Angela stay with an alcoholic husband?" she asked once the waiter had left.

Rob shook his head, obviously mystified by the situation. "She says she loves him. She isn't a quitter, you know. She's in it for the duration."

"No matter what you say?"

"Apparently," Rob replied. "My advice certainly has not been to stay with him."

"I see Angela five days a week now since I'm working at Wellspring Elementary for the rest of the year."

"That's a lengthy assignment for a sub, isn't it? How did that happen?" Rob asked.

"Maternity leave for the regular teacher. It makes it nice for me," she commented, looking at the dormant fireplace not far from their table. "I enjoy going to the same school every morning, getting to know the children, eating lunch with the same people...."

"If you like familiarity, why haven't you considered accepting a permanent position?"

"I've thought about it, but I haven't checked into it yet. I've only lived in Columbus for two years, and when I came here I wasn't sure how long I would stay. But I like it more than I ever thought I would."

"As a veteran of thirty-two years, I can say it's a great place to live."

"So I've discovered," Micah replied.

"What brought you here?"

Micah laughed softly as she considered her reasoning. "I was looking at a map, and I thought Columbus sounded like a good choice."

"A scientific approach," Rob remarked, smiling.

"I was living in Missouri at the time—Kansas City—and I knew it was time to move, but I—"

"Why was it time to move?" he interrupted.

"It was time," Micah said quietly. The past had come too close to touching her, but how could she explain that to him? "Sometimes you can just feel it."

Rob searched her face with inquisitive eyes, seeking answers she would not yet give. "Micah—"

"There were problems, family problems when I was a teenager," she stated in an unsteady voice. "I've been on my own since I was eighteen, and I've lived in quite a few places." There, she thought. I've said it. Said something, although Micah knew it would not be enough. Averting her gaze, she took a sip of water.

Rob studied her silently for a moment. "Eighteen is very young to be on your own. It couldn't have been easy."

"I got used to it," she answered truthfully. "Most kids leave home after high school anyway, to get jobs, go to college, whatever...."

"How did you get through college?"

"I worked. Secretarial jobs during the day, waitressing on the weekends. And I earned all the credits I could through a University Without Walls program in the evenings."

Rob watched her as she explained.

"When I'd finished all the courses I could in that program, I left my office job and waited tables in the evenings so I could attend daytime classes."

"When did you study?"

"Whenever I could. Breaks on the job, during meals, sometimes when I should have been sleeping," she said. "It was difficult, but I made it. I'm a teacher."

"So you are," Rob agreed. "And a very good one, too, according to my sister. I understand the kids love you."

"They're a fun bunch of kids to work with."

"Micah, where are you from originally?"

"California. A small town not far from Sacramento," she replied as the waiter brought a loaf of sourdough bread to the table with their salads. Micah was glad for the interruption. Talk about hometowns made her even more nervous than the disturbing warmth she found in Rob's eyes.

Time passed quickly as they spoke of the city and their hobbies and a dozen different things. Micah wondered if she would ever work her way to the bottom of the heaping bowl of fresh garden greens. So the talk about her hometown and the past was tabled, at least temporarily. For that, she was grateful. And the conversation they should have been having was forgotten in the midst of their laughter. They weren't good for each other, she knew. So why did it feel so right?

"That was a delicious meal, Rob," she said and slipped her arm through his as they exited the restaurant more than an hour later. "That bread was wonderful."

"I'm glad you liked it." Rob opened the car door for her. "How about a movie?"

"But there's something we need to discuss," Micah reminded him. "You said you'd let me explain why we can't—"

"Couldn't you explain it to me just as well after the movie?" It seemed the discussion could wait, but the film could not. The movie they wanted to see was due to start in thirty minutes, and they were nearly fifteen minutes from the theater.

Rain clouds threatened when they entered the show, and they found an actual downpour when they came out, one comedy and two boxes of popcorn later.

"I'll bring the car around to pick you up," Rob said as they stood under the theater's awning.

"No, it's not far. Let's run for it."

"It's pouring. You'll get soaked," Rob protested.

"You're just afraid I can beat you to the car," she dared him. Before he could respond, Micah stepped out into the rain, pulling her suit jacket over her head to cover part of her hair, and they both ran through the chilly downpour. Their laughter rose above the heavy pull of the sheets of water drenching them. They reached the car simultaneously, opened the doors and climbed in quickly.

"You should have locked your car!" Micah exclaimed. "It could have been stolen."

"But aren't you glad I didn't? We'd still be standing out there if I had," Rob answered.

Their laughter filled the automobile, and Rob wiped the rain from his face.

"How can you run in those shoes?" he asked, watching as Micah pushed wet strands of hair from her cheeks. She worked her fingers through it, untangling what she could.

"I was surprised that I could," she said, breathing hard from the exhilarating run. "If I had my tennis shoes on, I'd have had a better chance of outrunning you."

Rob's response came rather smugly. "Don't count on it."

The smile faded from Micah's face when she looked up at him. In that moment, she realized she didn't want to outrun him anymore. And the deep green of her eyes mirrored her thoughts.

The laughter faded from Rob's voice. The car seemed small; they were so close. Micah wiped a trickle of rain from her cheek, feeling the furious pounding of her heart in rhythm with the rain that fell on the roof, cutting them off from the world and shielding them with a wet curtain of privacy.

"Micah..." Rob spoke her name quietly, and it sounded lovelier than it ever had before. Then he leaned slowly toward her, and when his mouth touched hers, it was warm and undemanding, as though he expected her to pull away. But she did not. Rob was kissing her and although she had not wanted to admit it, that was what she had wanted almost from the first moment she met him.

She moved closer to him, placing a hand tentatively against his chest to brace herself and returned his kiss with newly discovered longing.

A sharp crack of lightning caused Micah to jump.

Rob smiled. She could feel the curve of his mouth against her own before the kiss ended.

"Afraid of lightning?" he whispered as they leaned together, forehead to forehead.

Micah smiled, too, with her eyes closed, while she enjoyed the flow of Rob's breath across her cheeks.

"No. I like storms," she answered. The lightning flashed again.

Rob turned to glance out the window. "Looks like it's slacking up enough to drive home."

Micah nodded. The storm did seem to be calming down a little, but the rapid beating of her heart was not. "Yes, it has," she agreed, pulling her wet hair away from her neck and letting it fall down the back of her jacket.

Rob started the engine and maneuvered the car away from the curb. The ride home was quiet. Micah spent most of her time staring out the window, watching the lightning grow farther and farther away in the distance.

The rain had picked up in intensity again when they pulled into the last available parking space in front of Micah's apartment.

"It's been a lovely evening," Micah said in a soft voice while she busied herself buttoning her jacket, purposely avoiding Rob's gaze.

"Micah," he began, drawing her attention to the serious blue of his eyes.

Her mouth felt dry and she swallowed hard. Clasping her hands together in front of her to keep them from fidgeting, she waited for his words.

But looking into the wide green eyes that viewed him so cautiously must have changed Rob's mind because he didn't speak right away. Instead, he touched her cheek tenderly.

"I have to be at school early in the morning," she managed to say while staring into his questioning eyes.

He studied her expression, one of half confusion and half fear, and his smile alleviated some of both. "All right, Micah," he replied quietly. "Maybe some other time."

And maybe not, she thought as she reached for the car door, not waiting for him to open it for her. This would be the end of it; it must be.

"Wait...." His warm hand rested on her left arm. "Don't go." His words were spoken so softly and with such tenderness, they nearly melted her heart...and her reasoning. Rob's hand moved up her arm to her shoulder and gently he pulled her toward him, into his arms. And when they came together, it was with the same longing she had experienced earlier. But now, their deepening kiss caused Micah to want more and more until—

"Rob." She gasped for breath, pulling away from him. "I have to go in—"

"Don't run away," he said in a gentle tone. "Don't be afraid of me."

"I'm not, it's just that—" Micah stopped. She should have told him goodbye last night. Would he ever understand that everything in her life was temporary? She opened the car door, but he reached across her and pulled it shut. Rain trickled down the inside of it.

"You are afraid," he answered quietly, "but there's no reason to be."

She knew instinctively she could trust this man although she did not understand why. "I don't want anything to happen," she insisted.

"Then nothing will," he replied. "I know what it means to be a Christian, Micah. When I said I was one years ago, it was real."

She looked over at him only to find a distant look in his eyes, and she waited for his explanation.

"I just couldn't go on with it forever...the way you can."

"But why? If it was real once, you know it can be again."

Rob shook his head, but not as emphatically as he could have, Micah noted with hopefulness. Then he continued. "Not now. Maybe someday if I could feel that trust again. But the point to this conversation is that I know you shouldn't be dating a non-believer, and you probably wouldn't have even gone out with me under ordinary circumstances."

"Probably not," she admitted. "But when Mr.

Lacey had his heart attack and we were there…everything happened so quickly. It seemed logical to want to talk more with you. How could I have known that by the time dinner was over, I'd feel this way about you? I mean, Rob, it was just pancakes!''

"That seemed innocent enough, didn't it?" Rob commented and laughed gently at her words. Then he touched her chin, tenderly turning her focus back to his eyes. "Do you hear what you're saying, Micah? You feel this as strongly as I do."

"Yes, but…I don't know what to say. We can't keep on seeing each other. It won't work."

"It can work. I don't believe all the things that you believe, but I won't stand in your way. Go to church, be the Christian you ought to be, love God more than anyone if that's how it has to be. But don't run away from what we could have together."

Chills ran through her. Her clothes were still damp and she shivered. She could have opened the door to go, but she found herself more drawn to him than ever by his tenderness. "Rob, I want us to be honest with each other, and the truth is, I left California to get away from my family. I have a mother who doesn't love me, a father I never see and no one else. I'm probably not a good risk for anyone's future, but especially not yours. My father—" She stopped.

He waited for a moment, then asked, "Your father…what?"

"He worked for a successful company near Sacramento. Things didn't go right. He's been in trouble with the law, and my mom moved away because of it. I guess I did, too."

"What did he do?"

"It doesn't matter. The important thing is that you understand a future with me would mean nothing but problems for you. Who knows? You could become a partner at Alsmore, Barlett and Maine one day or go into politics to become a judge. But with me..."

"Specifics, Micah. Why would having you in my life hurt my future?"

"You don't want anyone who comes from my family tree."

"I don't just want someone who comes from your family tree, Micah. I want you. And, unless you can look me in the eyes and honestly tell me you don't feel the same about me, I'm not walking away from this."

Micah averted her gaze to look out the window. She could not do what he asked, and he knew it as surely as she did.

"Don't be afraid of 'us,'" he said, touching her damp curls.

"It's not what you think it is."

"Then tell me what it is."

Micah had never come close to sharing her secrets with anyone until that moment, looking into Rob's warm eyes. But she had not moved all those miles, halfway across the country, only to tell the story again. She shook her head, her hair moving against her shoulders.

Rob searched her troubled expression and sorrowful green eyes that reflected painful memories. "Did someone hurt you?" he asked hesitantly.

"No, nothing like that," she answered. But the remarks and gossip a decade ago had stung almost as though it had been a physical affliction. "Rob, I can't talk about this. Not now—" Her voice broke off.

He nodded. "All right, when you're ready."

But Micah sensed there would be some things she'd never be ready to discuss. Not with Rob.

"I should go," she stated softly, turning to leave.

"I'll walk you to the door."

"No," she protested. "You have a long drive home. If you get out in this rain, you'll get drenched again."

"C'mon, let's go," he said and opened his car door.

"But there's no reason—"

Rob disregarded Micah's argument and came around to open her door. "You're not walking through that dark courtyard by yourself." He took one of her hands in his, and they hurried through the rain to the gate and back toward the rear apartment.

Micah slid the key into the lock and they stepped

inside the doorway, out of the stormy spring weather.

"Thank you, but I walk through that courtyard alone nearly every evening."

"You shouldn't," he stated. "You need an apartment that isn't so secluded."

She switched on the light in her not-so-tidy living room. Paints and brushes were scattered on top of her old coffee table and an easel sat in front of the window.

"Thank you for dinner...the movie...everything," she said.

"I want to see you again."

"No, Rob, please, let it go."

"I won't." Rob's warm hand brushed her face, tilting her chin up, and he studied the glimpse of honesty Micah had unknowingly shown him in a lingering gaze. "Tomorrow?"

Mixed feelings ran through her at the sound of his words. Another evening with him. What would it mean? Would it really matter so much? "Rob, we shouldn't."

"But we will," he stated bluntly.

"You're the one who will be hurt."

"I'll take my chances," he responded, and kissed her lightly on the temple. "Seven o'clock?"

"No, I have a class to teach at the tech school tomorrow evening. I'll be home around seven-thirty."

"That's not so late. I could come by then for a

while," he commented with a hint of a smile returning. He hesitated for a moment, and Micah thought he might kiss her again. But he made no move to touch her. "Tomorrow," he said as he slipped away from her, through the door into the rainy evening.

Micah closed the door and leaned against it. This was going in the wrong direction…and quickly.

The next day passed slowly for Micah as she silently berated herself throughout the hours for agreeing to see Rob again. More time spent with him would only make her want him more. But her heart was still winning out in the decision-making process when day turned to evening.

Rob arrived at exactly half past seven. Micah had returned home from class only minutes earlier, and she excused herself to change clothes.

"Could I use your phone to call my brother while you are changing? He left a message for me at work today asking me to call and, so far, I haven't been able to reach him."

"Sure, go ahead," Micah replied before disappearing into the bedroom and slipping out of her slacks and blouse and into a sky blue top and a soft, summery skirt splashed with color. She slid both feet into her favorite leather sandals and was walking from the bedroom back to the living room while running a brush through her free-flowing hair when she overheard part of Rob's telephone conversation.

"Yes, you can use the boat. I'm going to be too busy this weekend anyway. No, I had dinner with Liz tonight. Right. We had a good time. Sure, no problem. I'm at Micah's apartment now. See you later."

Micah stood in the doorway, and Rob replaced the receiver and looked up at her. "Ready? I thought we could go out for coffee and dessert."

Dessert. He had obviously already had dinner. With Liz.

"Micah?" he said when she failed to respond.

She forced a smile. "Fine. That sounds fine." Then she picked up the sweater she had left on the sofa. So what if there was a Liz? Micah had no future with him anyway. What had she expected?

"There's a little restaurant a few blocks from here that's famous for its strawberry pie. Does that sound good?"

"Yes, it's fine," she replied, wondering why her mind had gone so blank that "fine" was the only adjective she could think of. Other than "jealous."

They left her apartment and walked the few short blocks to the corner café where pie and coffee awaited them. Once seated in a semiprivate booth in the corner, Rob placed their order and studied the distant look in Micah's eyes.

"You're not talking much this evening. Did you have a bad day?" he inquired.

"No." The day had been good. It was the night

that was falling apart. "How about you?" she asked politely.

"What's wrong, Micah? Something has happened."

"No, it's nothing."

"We said we'd be honest," Rob reminded her. "It was your idea."

The waitress appeared with their food. Rob thanked her, then returned his attention to Micah, who sat staring into the swirl of cream she had poured into her coffee.

Honesty. It really had been her idea. "How was your dinner?" she asked in an artificially even tone. She knew it was none of her business, but the question would give her no peace.

"Dinner?" he responded with a frown. "Good. Fun. Why?"

He was going to make this difficult. She could see that in his casual reply.

"Just wondered."

"Liz called and said she was free for dinner and I was, too, so—"

"You can be free now, too, if you want to be. I told you we shouldn't see each other again," she said softly, being careful not to show any emotion. "You didn't need to cut your other plans short to keep this late date with me."

Rob had every right to be angry, and Micah fully expected to be informed that this was none of her business. But there was no sign of anger evident. In fact, Micah thought she saw a glimpse of a smile as he raised the coffee cup to his mouth before responding.

"You don't know who Liz is, do you?" he commented, a definite smile now curving his lips.

"Is there any reason I should?" She studied her untouched dessert. Even strawberry pie didn't look good. What was this man doing to her?

"You've worked with her every day this week."

Micah looked up at him in blank surprise.

"Angela Elizabeth," he stated.

"Your sister?" A warm blush of embarrassment colored her cheeks, and she raised a hand to her mouth. "I didn't know...I mean...you call her Liz?"

"I have since I was old enough to know she preferred being called Angela. Teasing that has stuck over the years." Rob reached across the small table, covering Micah's hand with his own. "Feel better?"

"Better?" she moaned. "I feel like a fool. I thought—"

"A little jealousy is good for a relationship," he replied and released her hand. "Now, eat your pie."

After several minutes of discussing the events of their workdays, Rob began a new line of conversation which surprised Micah almost as much as finding out who Liz was. It was about his past. And Nick.

"I remember coming in here for lunch occasionally, with Nick, years ago. The strawberry pie was the main attraction. Well, that and a pretty blond waitress.''

"That you liked?" Micah stuck a fork into a berry and raised it to her mouth.

Rob shook his head. "Nick. He fell in love with her.''

Nick. Rob's friend who had died, Micah recalled. The link between the man Rob is now and who he used to be. She put down the fork. "What happened?" she asked quietly.

"She died with him in the accident." Rob stared into his coffee cup, and Micah knew he was avoiding her gaze. She sat silently, uncertain whether or not to pursue the subject. Finally, she offered, "You still miss him.''

And Rob met her eyes, the stern look Micah glimpsed suddenly softening. "I always will.''

Micah nodded. She understood how that pain felt. "Always" could be a very long time. She placed her hand around the warm cup, hoping Rob would continue. And he did.

"Nick and Rachel had gone to hear a missionary they both knew speak in Cincinnati. They started home after the service. It had been raining...the roads were slick. And, in the dark, in the drizzle...he missed a curve.''

Micah's heart ached for the loss. Rob's. Nick and Rachel's. She watched him avert his gaze to look out the nearby window.

"They hit a tree and died. Just that quickly, Micah. He made a mistake, and they both died."

She listened without comment...and waited.

"Nick is...was the finest Christian I've ever known. He didn't deserve to die so young...and not like that. What a senseless loss."

"Yes, it is," she agreed softly. "I don't know why so many things happen that we don't understand."

Rob glanced back into Micah's eyes with a critical look. "Neither do I. At the funeral I asked the district superintendent how something like this could happen. To *Nick* of all people. He loved the Lord and tried to serve Him how he knew best. And yet, he was dead. So, what do you suppose the D.S.'s answer was?"

Micah gave a slight shrug of her shoulders. "I don't know."

"That's it. 'I don't know,'" Rob gave a harsh laugh. "'I don't know,'" he repeated, running a hand through his hair in a restless movement. "What kind of an answer was that for the deaths of two good people?"

"An honest one."

"An *inadequate* one," Rob retorted. "And I knew I was about to plunge into a *world* of inadequate answers...a *lifetime* of them."

"That's what faith is all about, Rob. None of us will get very far in this life without it."

"I didn't have enough. Not then, not now."

Micah weighed her words carefully. "Nick was your best friend. He wouldn't want his death to cost you your relationship with the Lord. I think it would break his heart to know that about you."

"Knowing Nicholas Alsmore the way I did, I'm sure you're right." Rob's eyes flashed an angry glance, and he signaled for their check.

"Alsmore? Of Alsmore, Barlett and Maine? Your law firm?"

"One and the same," he responded, pulling several bills from his wallet. "Nick was the son of Taylor Alsmore, the senior partner. He had planned to become a lawyer." Rob rose from his seat in the booth and held out his hand to Micah.

She took the hand extended and stood up to leave with him. "And now you work with Nick's dad…in place of Nick…."

"No one can replace Nick," Rob remarked while opening the door to exit the restaurant. "But, yes, I work with his dad."

They stepped out onto the brick sidewalk and began to walk the several blocks to Micah's apartment, hand in hand, and Micah couldn't remember such a simple pleasure meaning so much. She walked silently by his side, knowing she could have held his hand forever, through lack of faith, loss of friends, days of thunder and lightning or sunshine. Forever. And the thought terrified her. She needed to think about something else. Anything else. Maybe Rob would talk more about his past.

"Do you work with Alsmore because you want to, or because you think you should?" She asked the question that nagged at her.

"The shoulds and the oughts make a lot of demands on us, don't they?" he replied and squeezed her hand. "It's a good job, Micah. The money is great, the future looks promising...."

A stab of guilt pierced her heart. She was enjoying the present far too much to consider the future. His or hers. And she wanted to know more about his past.

"Rob, tell me about Nick. What was he like?"

"We grew up on the same street, started kindergarten and went all through school together." He smiled. "We played army and cops and robbers after school. Then came Little League, and junior-high basketball. We both learned to drive the same summer." Rob stopped speaking, and Micah walked along with him in silence.

"I'm trying to think how to describe him. Confident, I guess, and happy...funny...self-disciplined...optimistic...a good judge of people. He'd have made a great lawyer."

Too soon they reached their destination, and Rob swung open the black wrought-iron gate. They entered, walking through the courtyard to Micah's front door.

"Rachel always said Nick was a gentleman. I think that's a good word for him."

Micah unlocked the door, and they stepped inside.

"Then Nick was a lot like you," she offered, looking up at the warmth she knew she'd find in his eyes.

Rob took Micah easily into his arms, gently pulling her close. "You've reminded me to be a gentleman at a most inopportune moment, you know."

"Sorry." She whispered the insincere apology with a tender smile.

"Me, too," Rob responded, the words nearly smothered as his mouth descended to meet hers in a kiss that slowly weakened every fiber of Micah's resolve. But, too soon, Rob pulled away, brushing her forehead with a tender "Good night." Then he stepped out into the courtyard again and was gone. With no mention of tomorrow.

Chapter Five

"Hi, stranger," Carole said when Micah walked into the otherwise empty beauty salon. "I was just cleaning up. Want to get a sandwich with me?"

"Sure. I didn't have a chance to eat after school. I am kind of hungry."

"Kind of? I'd think you'd be starved. It's almost nine o'clock."

Micah shook her head. She hadn't had much of an appetite lately. Not since the strawberry pie.

"So, how's your attorney?" Carole's brown eyes flashed with mischief as she looked up from the sink she was rinsing.

"He's not *my* attorney, or my anything apparently," Micah replied quietly. She turned down the air conditioner the way she knew Carole did at closing time. "Are you ready to go?"

Carole shut off the water faucet. "I thought you and Rob were doing fine together."

"Not exactly," came Micah's soft reply.

"Why not?" Carole persisted. "What happened?"

"I haven't heard a word from him for eight days."

"But who's counting, right?" Carole frowned and started sweeping the floor. "That seems so odd. I really thought you had a thing going."

Micah shook her head and reached for the dustpan to hand it to Carole. "Are you almost ready?"

"What did you do to scare him away?" Carole asked bluntly while ignoring Micah's question. "Tell him about your dislike for the legal profession? I swear, Micah, if you don't stop being so paranoid—"

"No," she interrupted. "Nothing like that. I mean, we had really nice times together. At least, I thought we did. We ate dinner at my apartment that first night. I tried to tell him that I wouldn't be good for him, but he refused to listen. He said he was willing to take that chance. And we've been together two other evenings."

"Three dates in a row? Then nothing?"

Micah nodded, not trusting her wavering voice with a reply.

"Wow," Carole commented. "What did you say to him?"

"We've talked about all kinds of things, but nothing that would explain this."

"Did you get too preachy with him about your Christianity? You have a way of doing that, you know."

"No, I didn't. Actually, he brought up the subject. And if I seem pushy about it, that's because it's important to me. I certainly don't want a future with someone who doesn't share my beliefs, and I shouldn't even date anyone who doesn't."

"What harm could dating someone like—"

"If I date a man like that, I could fall in love with him. Then what? Ask him to change? Get him converted?"

Carole shook her head, admitting defeat. "I get your point. But what about Rob?"

"He was a Christian when he was younger, but then something happened and he left the church."

"So he's got two strikes against him—his future clashes in some way with your past *and* he's a nonbeliever. If the picture looks that bleak, why do you care that he's not called? Why not just let him go?"

"Because..." Micah caught her lower lip between her teeth when warm tears filled her eyes.

Carole froze in her steps, studying her friend's troubled expression. "You really like this guy, don't you?"

"I didn't want to, but—"

"But you do. You really do."

Micah nodded again. "Too much, too soon."

Carole gave her a generous hug. "You can't possibly care too much. The more the better! And it's certainly not too soon. You're twenty-eight years old, and I haven't seen you serious about anyone in the two years I've known you. I'd say you're long overdue for a full-fledged romance."

"It takes two to make a romance," Micah commented. "I thought Rob—"

"Don't give up on him yet. Maybe he's just busy with work or something else."

"Or some*one* else."

"No, now, let's think positive. Maybe he's been sick with the flu or had an accident."

"Right, Carole. Positive thinking at its best," Micah quipped and opened the front door.

"Well, I'm sorry. I'm just trying to be helpful. Let's go get some food and we'll devise a plan to rekindle his interest."

But the only plan Micah would agree to was to wait. If Rob wanted to see her, he would call. And if he didn't, she thought she might die.

Busy with a trial. The message glared at her from the pink While You Were Out note stuck on her desk when she returned to her classroom after supervising lunch in the cafeteria the next day. Micah crumpled the paper with more force than necessary and tossed it into the nearby trash can.

An excuse phoned in to the Wellspring Elementary School office while Micah was busy with the kids. "Nice knowing you, Counselor," she murmured as she slammed her books into a disorderly stack. Hot tears burned her eyes and she blinked hard, not wanting them to fall. But it was better this way. She shouldn't have dated him at all. Maybe finally he had listened to her warning and decided he didn't want to take the risk. She couldn't blame him for that. He had a lot at stake. "But at least you could have told me in person, not leave a message with a twelve-year-old office volunteer at the school," she thought aloud.

"Hey, Micah?" Angela burst into the classroom with an abundance of energy. "Heather's with her grandmother, I'm taking the boys for ice cream and we wondered if you'd like to go along."

Micah pulled a tissue from the box she kept on her desk. "Thanks, but—"

"What's wrong? Are you okay?" Angela noticed Micah's reddened eyes. "Did something happen?"

"I'm all right," she responded and blew her nose. "But I really don't feel like eating ice cream." The threatening tears subsided, and Micah was grateful.

"Trouble with a student?"

"No," she answered as she picked up her sweater from the back of her swivel chair. "It's just…there's been a misunderstanding. I really thought that…"

"Thought what? Does this have anything to do with Rob?" Angela asked hesitantly.

Micah glanced up at Angela, who stood awkwardly inside the doorway, apparently unsure whether to stay or go.

"I'm a pretty good listener, Micah, if you want to talk. If not, I'll understand."

"He's your brother. I can't talk about him with you."

"Nonsense. I'm his sister, not his spy. This can be confidential," Angela replied. "But if you'd rather not—"

"No, it's okay. It's just that, well, you know we went out several times. I thought we both enjoyed it, but—"

"Why would you doubt that? What did he say?" Angela asked.

"Nothing." Micah gathered her belongings and walked toward the doorway. "That's the mystery. Everything seemed fine after our last date. Then, nothing. I haven't heard from him in more than a week, except for a message called in to the school office explaining that he was busy."

"Busy? That's all he said?" Angela stepped into the hallway with Micah. "That doesn't sound like Rob."

"'Busy with a trial' was the actual message. But, unless times have changed, court is not in session in the evenings or on weekends."

"I haven't seen him lately myself, but we've spent so much time moving into our new house, he may have called and I missed it. I'll try to reach him tonight."

"If you do talk to him, don't mention any of this. I don't want him to feel that he owes me an explanation."

"Why not? He does owe you one."

The two women walked out into the bright sunshine. "But three dates don't exactly add up to a relationship." Did they? No, it wasn't really the dates that caused Micah to believe they had something special. It was Rob's gentle touch and the tenderness in his eyes that had promised more than she had known with any man. Had her heart been wrong?

Chapter Six

The knocking on the door woke Micah from a restless sleep. The illuminated dial of the alarm clark showed 2:00 a.m. *Bang, bang, bang.* Before she walked from the bedroom, she grabbed the sweatpants she had left in the nearby chair and pulled them on under the big T-shirt she wore as a nightgown.

"Who is it?" she called in a sleep-filled voice, reaching for the light switch and running a hand through her tousled hair.

"It's me."

She froze. "Rob?" Ten days had passed since she had last seen him. Ten days with nothing more than a telephone message. Micah pulled open the front door. "It's 2:00 a.m."

"I know it's late," he began, "but I just left the office—"

"The office? In the middle of the night?"

"I need to see you."

Micah stood speechless for a moment, staring into the eyes that had haunted her nights and unsettled her days. "It's been a long time," she said in a voice much calmer than she felt.

"I've tried to call. We've been in trial—"

"Did Angela ask you to come?" she asked, remembering the conversation she'd had with her friend the other day. She should never have confided in someone so close to Rob.

"Angela?" he asked with a frown. "What does my sister have to do with us?"

Micah shook her head slowly. "Nothing...." Nothing, she hoped.

Rob remained outside the door, his hands sunk into the pockets of his slacks. "Let me explain."

"There's no need for excuses, Rob."

"Excuses?" he responded sharply. "Do you think I'd come here at this hour to give you excuses?"

"I don't know." Her reply came softly. "I don't know what to expect from you."

He looked away from her, into the dark courtyard, as his anger seemed to fade. "It's this trial, Micah. It's a nightmare." He paused, looking once again into her doubtful gaze. "We've spent every spare moment rehashing the case in Alsmore's office. Last weekend I had to fly to Phoenix to interview the client's brother for more details, and I was stuck out there for three days trying to locate the guy.''

Mrs. Poe's upstairs light came on, and Micah and Rob both glanced up at the tiny window to the east of the small rear apartment. Their privacy came to an annoying end when the landlady peered out at them from behind the shade.

''Come in,'' Micah offered, opening the door a little wider.

''Why don't you have an answering machine?'' he asked as he stepped inside.

''They're so impersonal,'' she replied. ''Besides, I didn't think I could justify the expense.''

''I've tried to call from the office, but you're never here. And it's been one or two o'clock in the morning before I get home each day. I didn't want to call you so late.''

Rob stepped inside as he spoke, and Micah closed the door, leaning against it for a moment. Was this just an excuse? And did it really matter? Ten days or one hundred, she had missed him.

''Micah?'' Rob touched her shoulder.

She turned abruptly and pulled away from the contact. ''So,'' she began in an unsteady voice, ''the trial is going badly?'' Micah cleared her throat nervously and walked away from him.

''Yes,'' he answered, studying her restless movement. ''Very.''

''Do you...do you want to talk about it?'' Was that why he was here? What did he want from her?

She sat down on the arm of the couch, not too close, not too far away.

"No." Rob sank into the sofa's worn cushions. His voice, already scratchy and slightly hoarse, grew quiet. "That's all I've talked about for days."

His tone sounded low and remote, tired and unfamiliar; and it had been so long. Reaching out, almost without thinking, Micah traced a finger down the thin, shadowy line of his unshaven cheek. Seeing the weariness in his eyes, it was easy to forget the rights and the wrongs, the should be's and shouldn't be's.

"You look exhausted," she said, whisper-soft. "And you must be hungry."

"Only for the sight of you," he replied, capturing her hand in a slow, steady movement. Then, raising it to his lips, he pressed a kiss to her palm. Micah thought her heart would stop beating at the feel of his soft touch against her skin.

"Ten days..." Rob's eyes lowered to her lips, softly parted in unspoken response, and his voice was as gentle as a warm caress. "I'd almost forgotten how beautiful you are."

Ten days. He had counted, and tears filled her eyes. "Oh, Rob," she murmured, sliding easily into his arms. He held her close, breathing in the fragrance of her hair.

"Missed me?" he whispered.

Micah nodded, her cheek rubbing against the soft fabric of his shirt. "So much."

"Good," he replied before kissing the crown of her head. "I'd hate to think I was the only one who was miserable these past ten days."

She dried her tears on the sleeve of her T-shirt. "When you didn't call, I thought that—" She broke off raggedly.

"That I didn't want to see you?" He cupped her face in his hands. "You can't mean that."

Micah's mouth turned down in a sorrowful curve. She did mean it; she hadn't known. For ten days and nights, she had not known. "The last time we were together, you said nothing about the next day or the weekend or—"

"Do I need to say those things to you?" He touched the corner of her frown with a warm thumb. "Don't you know I want to be with you? Tomorrow and the next day and the next..."

No, she hadn't known—until now.

Rob's hand slid into the soft curls at the base of her neck, pulling her slowly, gently, toward him. Micah came willingly, her fingers touching the collar of his shirt. As his mouth met hers, the empty days of waiting faded, and the memories of her aching uncertainty dimmed in this meeting of their hearts.

Micah raised one hand to feel the slight roughness of his cheek beneath her fingertips as Rob abandoned her lips for the smooth line of her jaw and the curve of her neck. But when his mouth brushed the rapid pulse pounding in the slender column of her throat, he hesitated.

"Micah." Her name was whispered, warm and lovely against her skin.

"Hmm..." She could barely think when he was touching her.

"Honey," Rob began, his hands tightening on her shoulders, and he raised his head to look into trusting green eyes flecked with gold. The hesitation was gone, replaced by certainty. "Would you make some coffee?"

"Coffee?" Micah's wide-eyed gaze asked more than her one-word question. Had she heard him correctly?

"I came here to see you, to be with you, Micah," he said, then kissed her forehead lightly, his lips lingering against the pleasant taste of her skin. "Not to take advantage of a sleepy young woman."

A blush colored her cheeks, and she stared down at the open collar of Rob's shirt. She had dreamed of him, of being in his arms this way; but she hadn't imagined it ending with a cup of coffee.

"Micah, please," he stated firmly.

She nodded, a little stunned by the interruption. "Coffee," she repeated and stood up on wobbly legs.

Opening a cupboard door in the kitchen, she stood staring at the contents until she could think clearly again. Then she saw the bread. "Would you like a sandwich? I have ham salad."

"That sounds great," Rob answered as he entered the kitchen and leaned against the counter, watching her.

"And I have iced tea, unless you really do want coffee?"

"Tea would be fine," he responded with a disturbing smile. "Where were you all day?"

"Out in the country working on my painting of the church. There's something about that place that keeps me wanting to go back again and again."

"Maybe you should attend there if you feel that strongly about it," he suggested.

"I'd like that, but it's such a long drive," she commented. "Would you go with me once? Just to see it?"

"Yes," he agreed. "I will."

She smiled. "Anyway, when I came home from painting, Carole and I went out to dinner and to a play. I didn't get home until after midnight."

"I called at least a dozen times today." He took the glass that Micah offered him and placed it on the counter. "And every evening this week. Don't you ever stay home?"

Micah cut the sandwich she was working on in half and placed the plate next to Rob's glass on the counter. "I've been home off and on, but I taught adult evening art classes several nights, and I did some private tutoring at a student's home."

"Didn't you get the message I left at school?"

"Yes." She remembered how much it had hurt

to read the note. A called-in excuse reminiscent of a phoned-in prescription at the pharmacy. Impersonal, brief, necessary. "You were busy with a trial."

"I didn't say that. I told the student who answered the phone that I was in trial and couldn't leave a number where I could be reached. I asked that you call me at home that night after midnight."

Micah returned the leftover ham salad to the refrigerator shelf with a thud. "She didn't tell me that part."

"Did she tell you the part about how I can barely sleep for thinking about you?" Rob took a drink of the iced tea while watching Micah's face register surprise at his statement.

"Rob, surely you didn't say that to a student?"

He shook his head, his eyes dancing with amusement as he returned the tea to the counter. "No, but maybe she would have remembered the message more accurately if I had."

"Kids do have a way of remembering things they shouldn't have heard," she said softly and moved into his arms. Her voice lowered to a gentle whisper. "And you're not the only one who's had trouble sleeping, you know."

"No, I didn't know," he replied, his darkening eyes searching her unsmiling face. His arms closed around her with hands strong and firm against her waist. "I thought you said you didn't look good in yellow?"

Micah's gaze lowered momentarily to the yellow T-shirt and then raised once again to study the serious slant of Rob's mouth. "I didn't think anyone would see me wearing this old T-shirt. I'm not in the habit of letting people into my apartment at two o'clock in the morning."

"You'd better not be," he remarked in a harsh, uncompromising tone.

"Not even you, Counselor?" she teased.

The line of his mouth curved a little, giving way to a suppressed smile. "There are exceptions to every rule."

The light shining from Micah's clear gaze revealed that Rob was already the exception, to that rule and to others that governed her heart.

"It's been a long ten days, Micah." His hands slid up into the auburn curls that hung in disarray halfway down her back. "Go away with me tomorrow, just for the day."

"Where?" she asked, smiling. As if it mattered.

"Away from work, responsibility, humanity..."

"It's supposed to rain all day," she commented, remembering the weather forecast she had heard. But it could still be a perfect day. "You look so tired, Rob." Her fingers barely touched his unshaven cheek. "Why don't you get some sleep, then come back around noon. I'll be home from church by then. We could spend the rest of the day here."

"Here?" Rob studied her face curiously.

"I have plenty of food, and we could unplug the

phone so no one would bother us.'' Her voice grew softer as she spoke. "I love to be at home on dark, stormy days.''

"A rainy day in an apartment all to ourselves? That's a dangerous invitation you're issuing, Miss Shepherd.''

Micah knew it was. The whole relationship was dangerous, for both of them. Had she so easily forgotten the rationale that had consoled her during the days of his absence? That they were better parted than they could ever be together? "Maybe we're wrong,'' she said in a hushed tone, almost surprised to hear her inner fears spoken aloud. "Maybe—''

"Micah...'' Rob's voice remained hoarse, slightly husky as he tilted her chin up, forcing her to meet his gaze. Then his mouth, still moist from his last taste of iced tea, touched her lips in a kiss, light, provocative and deliberately unsatisfying. "Does it feel wrong to you?'' was the quiet question asked before the next contact, equally light and much too brief. No, nothing seemed wrong when she was in his arms. No thoughts, no maybes...only feelings. Feelings that she knew would not be enough to see them through. But her reply was lost as Rob's mouth met hers with the firm, slow kiss she longed for, and her gentle response only made it taste even sweeter and more tender than either had imagined.

What were these feelings stirring inside her? It was too soon for love. Much too soon.

"Micah..." Her name was softly spoken, and her eyes flew open at the ache in his voice. "I—"

She waited endless moments. Did he feel it, too?

"I'd better leave," he said so quietly she strained to hear his words.

Rob kissed her again, his mouth barely touching the soft hair at her temple. "I'll be back tomorrow...with the rain," he added without smiling. Then he walked away. Micah listened to the front door close behind him.

Standing in the aching loneliness of her kitchen, she traced a finger lightly across her lips, still warm from his kiss. She had waited all these years for love, real love. But it couldn't be found in the arms of a man she barely knew. Not now; not with Rob. The attorney. That's what Rob Granston was and what he would always be.

"Lord, how could this happen? I've been alone all these years but never really felt lonely until now, when I'm away from Rob. Why now? With this man I can't have?" She sighed and hugged her arms close to her.

She was twenty-eight years old. A grown woman. Had she learned nothing from the past? Nothing from her mother's warnings?

Chapter Seven

Micah pushed her pillow out of the way and grabbed the ringing phone.

"Good morning, sleepyhead," said the voice on the other end of the receiver.

"Hi. What time is it?" she asked, reaching for the clock.

"Seven-twenty."

"I like getting wake-up calls from you." Micah sat up in bed, pulling the sheet around her. "Are you coming over later?" She glanced out the window. "It will be raining soon."

"I don't have to wait for the rain to start, do I?" Rob asked.

She laughed and assured him she wanted to see him, regardless of the weather.

"I have some news," he offered, the tone of his voice suddenly serious.

"Good or bad?" She tucked a few curls behind her ear as she asked the needless question.

"Not good," he replied. "Our rainy-day plans together must be postponed."

"But, why? I thought you had the day off—"

"I do, but Liz's father-in-law was rushed to the hospital in the middle of the night. She and Dan went up to Cleveland to be with him, and since Mom and Dad are out of town and they couldn't find a sitter at five o'clock in the morning, they dropped the kids off here. I have three sleeping children in my apartment."

"Come anyway. Bring the kids. It will be fun, and it sounds like you might need help."

"Truth is, I'm used to having one or even two of them around sometimes on the weekend. But I'm not too good with all three at once. Are you sure you wouldn't mind?"

"I'm a teacher, remember? Three children won't exactly be a challenge. And I can stay home from church this morning."

"Heather's waking up. She just crawled off the couch and turned on the television."

"I have plenty of stuff for sandwiches, and I think I have some grapes and cookies. We can eat lunch here."

"I promised them French toast for breakfast, so I'd better go find the skillet."

"Really? I didn't know you cooked." Her teeth sank gently into her lower lip as she smiled. The more she learned about this man, the more she liked him.

"I don't much. But the kids are easily impressed. Anyway, they like to help crack the eggs."

"Uncle Rob, I'm hungry."

Micah laughed softly as she heard the little girl's voice in the background.

"Got to go. I'm being paged," he said. "See you in a couple of hours...if you're sure."

"I'm sure. Good luck with breakfast."

"Thanks. I'll need it."

Micah replaced the receiver slowly and got out of bed. She needed to check her cupboards to see if she had to make a quick run to the grocery store for anything before the arrival of her guests.

"We stay with Uncle Rob sometimes," David said with a hint of pride in his young voice that brought a quick smile to Micah's face. "And he lets us stay up real late."

A flash of lightning drew Micah's attention to the kitchen window. Her Sunday-afternoon plans for the three young strangers in her apartment were working out easily enough, despite the rain sliding down the windowpanes.

"That's on the weekend, David," Rob interjected. "If you stay with me tonight, you'll have an early bedtime because it's a school night."

Rob's comments brought no response as eight-year-old David busied himself setting up a game of Monopoly.

"Not like that." The older boy, Nathan, objected to David's methods of distributing the money. "Haven't you ever played this game before?"

"You got any cookies?" Heather asked as she followed Micah around the kitchen watching sandwiches being assembled.

"Rob, look up in that top cabinet, please," Micah said as she gently pulled the little girl's ponytail. "What's your favorite kind, honey?"

"Oatmeal," Rob replied, glancing mischievously at Micah.

"I was speaking to the child," Micah replied, faking a frown of displeasure.

"Chocolate chip!" Heather exclaimed. "Those are my favorites. Only Uncle Rob likes the oatmeal kind."

Rob handed the package of cookies he found in the top cabinet to Micah.

"You'll be happy to know these are chocolate chip," Micah said. "Uncle Rob is out of luck this time, Heather."

"That's a matter of opinion," came Rob's response.

Micah handed one cookie to the little girl and glanced up at Rob with questioning eyes. Just as Rob leaned forward to kiss her, the boys had a difference of opinion themselves.

"It's my turn, dummy. I told you—"

"Hey, guys! No name-calling." Rob's attention turned to the argument coming from the living room. "I think you need a referee in there," he said, disappearing around the corner.

"Can I have another cookie?" Heather asked.

"Not right now, sweetheart. After lunch." Micah looked at her small table and the four accompanying chairs. "Maybe we'll have an indoor picnic. Does that sound like fun?"

"Sure! How?" Heather asked.

"We'll spread out a sheet on the living-room floor and take all the food in there to eat."

"Okay! I'll tell Uncle Rob." Heather ran out of the kitchen.

Micah walked into her bedroom and opened the bottom drawer of her dresser to pull out a sheet.

"Are you sure you want these wild hooligans eating on your living-room carpet?"

Rob's voice startled her, and she rose up quickly. "They can't hurt anything," she said. "I'll put this sheet down to cover the carpet and that will catch most of the crumbs." She picked up the sheet. "When you don't have enough chairs to seat the number of guests invited, you have living-room picnics."

Heather came tagging along just moments behind her uncle. "Davy and Nathan are ready for the picnic."

Rob and Micah both laughed, and Rob leaned over to pick up his dark-haired niece. "But the picnic is not quite ready for them, babe. Let's go help Micah finish getting everything ready."

"She's pretty," Heather said as she peeked at Micah over Rob's shoulder.

"She sure is," Rob confirmed, carrying the child from the bedroom.

"And real nice, too," Heather added with a shy smile.

"You're pretty and nice yourself, Heather," Micah replied, and Heather buried her face in Rob's shoulder.

Rob turned to Micah when they entered the kitchen and kissed her lightly on the mouth.

"Yuck!" David had just stepped into the room. "Kissin'!"

"In a few years, you'll like it," Rob said, smiling as he sat Heather on the floor. But the look on David's face said he doubted his uncle's words. "Now, Micah's been very nice having us over here for lunch, so let's cooperate with her."

"That means 'help me,'" Micah explained as Heather looked at Rob with a puzzled expression. "Cooperate is kind of a big word, isn't it?"

"Thank you, Teacher."

"You're welcome, Counselor," Micah replied and picked up a couple of packages of fruit-flavored punch to pour into a pitcher on the counter. Counselor. That was the only flaw she had seen in him so far, and she refused to think about that today.

"Okay, move the board game. Nat, you missed a couple of pieces. Good...okay. Now, help me spread out this sheet. David, grab that corner. Nat, get the other one. Heather, hon, move out of the way."

Micah added sugar to the drinks and listened to the conversation in the living room. Rain beat upon the roof and poured down the windowpanes partly hidden by yellow and white curtains. Stirring the punch, she watched the rain through the glass, knowing that when it was quiet, she could hear the drops hitting the leaves on the apple tree outside the living room window.

Then the kitchen was invaded by three miniature helpers.

The potato chips went to Heather, the plates and cups to David and the silverware and napkins to Nathan, and they all carried their assigned item to the picnic area.

"You take the sandwiches," she said to Rob, "and I'll take the punch and the baked beans."

Micah followed her guests into the living room and arranged everything in as orderly a fashion as possible, using her large coffee table as a buffet.

Nathan wandered over to the couch and practiced his karate chops on the cushions.

"No martial arts during lunch, Nat. Come on." Rob steered him back to his seat on the floor.

"So, you like karate?" Micah asked, remembering Angela's concerns.

"Yep, sure do," Nathan replied as he plopped

down in his designated spot and began munching on a ham and cheese sandwich. "But Mom don't like me liking it."

"You try to chop up tables and stuff," David responded, shedding a little light on the subject.

"Maybe if you were more careful about what you practiced on, your mom wouldn't mind so much," Rob commented.

"Can I have another cookie?" Heather asked.

Micah looked over at the plate containing a sandwich with only two small bites missing. "Eat at least half your sandwich, then you may." And to Micah's amazement, the child complied without argument.

The picnic went smoothly and within a half hour or so, the boys were playing Monopoly again and Heather was watching a cartoon video she had brought with her on the VCR. Rob and Micah cleaned up the lunch dishes.

"They're good kids, Rob. Really," Micah added while putting the leftovers in the refrigerator.

"Yes, they are. Whenever the boys spend the weekend with me, we enjoy the time together. Heather won't come with us most of the time because we usually go boating or fishing and she's afraid of the water."

"That's too bad. She's missing a lot of fun."

"When you accompany us, maybe we can talk her into coming along. With you there, she might not be so afraid."

The phone rang.

"It's probably Angela," Micah said. "Go ahead and answer it." She wiped her hands on a dish towel and listened to Rob's voice grow cold and impersonal with the party on the other end of the receiver.

"May I tell her who's calling?" Whoever it was, it certainly wasn't Angela.

"Scott," Rob explained, handing the phone to her with a disapproving glance.

She hadn't heard from Scott in months. Hadn't wanted to. So why did he have to call now?

"Hello? Yes, hi, Scott. How have you been?"

"Is that Mommy?" Heather climbed down from the sofa and came running toward them.

"No," Rob answered. "Your mom will call soon. Let's watch some more cartoons until she does."

Scott had remembered that Micah liked stormy days. He had thought of her often. Law school wasn't going so well.

Micah spoke as politely as she could. Thanks, but no thanks. Yes. She was involved with someone else now. Scott wanted to see her anyway. Surely she wasn't so involved with someone that she wouldn't see anyone else. Her new relationship wasn't that serious, was it? Scott wanted to know.

Micah studied Rob's frowning expression where he sat on the couch with Heather cuddled up close to him. He glanced away from the television which had so captured his niece's attention and his eyes locked with Micah's for a brief, questioning moment.

"Yes," Micah answered Scott's question. "It is serious." Finally, wonderfully, dangerously serious.

She replaced the receiver and approached the couch, which now held not only Rob and Heather, but the other two kids, as well, while an old movie blared from the screen. The kids were so engrossed in the science fiction movie, they didn't notice when Micah leaned forward and kissed Rob on the cheek. His eyebrows rose as if to question her about the call, but she shook her head. "It wasn't important. Just a voice from the past," she explained.

"And he'd better remain there," Rob stated flatly.

"Shh!" three young voices chimed in.

Just a voice from the past. Micah shivered as she settled down into the space remaining on the couch cushions next to Heather. There were other voices from the past that, if they spoke, would not be so easily silenced.

The phone rang again shortly, and Nathan was off the couch in a moment's notice. "I'll get it." Then he stopped and looked at Micah. "Can I?"

"Sure," she answered and within seconds Nathan was talking to his mother on the other end of the line.

Rob asked Nathan for the phone. "Liz? Is everything all right? Sure...no problem. We'll be there soon. Bye."

"Is her father-in-law okay?" Micah asked.

"Yes. They were allowed to see him for only a

few minutes, but he looked good and his condition is stable.''

Micah glanced at Heather, who had fallen asleep on the couch. The boys, however, were as awake and lively as ever.

"Let's go, guys," Rob said. "Your folks are home and waiting for you."

"We want to finish the movie!" David responded. "We can't go now!"

Nathan asked, "Did they land on Mars yet?"

"Nope," David replied. "But they're gonna in a second."

Rob and Micah looked at each other, and Micah shrugged. "There's only about half an hour left of the show," she offered. "Why don't we let them finish it?"

So they sat down and watched the spaceship land while Heather slept soundly through a much-needed nap.

Later, getting everyone loaded into Rob's car took a while, with last-minute drinks and trips to the bathroom.

"All right, in the car, everybody. It's only a twenty-minute ride to your parents' home. You can drink and do whatever you need to do then!"

The kids thanked her for the picnic and good time they'd had without prompting from Rob, which both pleased and surprised their uncle.

"Be careful driving," she whispered to Rob and kissed him lightly, which brought giggles from the passengers. "It's going to start raining again soon. I can feel it."

"Sure you don't want to ride to Liz and Dan's with us?"

"I'm sure. You go ahead, and I'll take care of a few things around here. You'll be back soon?"

"Yes," he replied. "I will."

She pulled her sweater around her shoulders as cold raindrops began to fall once again, and she waved goodbye to the three youngsters waving to her from the rear window of Rob's car. She laughed softly at the sight. The argument over the front seat had been so intense, Rob had ordered them all into the back.

Micah hurried into the apartment when the rain turned into a downpour. There were surprisingly few things to pick up, and the lunch dishes had already been taken care of, so she had time for a quick shower. Then she slipped into a clean pair of jeans and a soft, cream-colored shirt.

Rain-spattering footsteps splashing through the courtyard caused Micah to hurry to the door, opening it wide.

"Come in," she called as Rob neared the entrance to her apartment. "The kids got home okay?"

He stepped inside the doorway, out of the drizzle and handed her a package. "Yes, and on the way there, I stopped at one of the one-hundred-flavor ice-cream stores."

"A hundred flavors! Rob, I think there are really only thirty or so."

"Whatever. It doesn't matter. If there were only two flavors, the kids would argue over it. I finally ended up buying a half gallon of some double-dutch chocolate or something like that for the boys to take home, and Heather wanted—"

"Mint chocolate chip?" Micah asked as she took Rob's rain-soaked jacket from him after setting the package on the floor.

Rob looked at her in obvious surprise. "How'd you know?"

"I've purchased ice-cream cones for dozens of kids at one time or another. She just looked like someone who might ask for the green minty kind."

"Thank you," Rob said quietly as Micah placed his jacket on a hanger and looked up at him. "I mean...for helping me with the kids, especially on such short notice."

"You're welcome. So what's in the package?"

"What flavor of ice cream might you ask for, Miss Shepherd?"

"Depends on the mood I'm in," she replied. "On a rainy day like this, I'd probably think something chocolate would be comforting."

"Lucky guess on my part," Rob said, pulling a half gallon of chocolate ice cream from the sack. "You'd better put this in the freezer before it melts."

"Thank you." Micah took the carton from his extended hands.

"Wait. There's something else in here for you." Rob pulled a square box about the size of a large telephone book from the bag. "There was an electronics store right next door to the ice-cream shop—"

"Electronics?"

"And they were having a sale on telephone answering machines."

"Answering machines? Rob, they're expensive. I can't accept—"

"Yes, you can. I would have gladly given the price of this machine several times over these past ten days to be able to get an accurate message to you. Do me and our conflicting schedules a favor and accept it."

Micah looked from the machine Rob was pulling from the cardboard box to the ice cream in her hands.

"Go ahead and put that away," Rob said, nodding toward the ice cream. "I'll hook up this thing and we'll see how it works."

She smiled and exited the living room. "Do you want any dinner?" she called from the kitchen. "I could make a pizza."

"No, thanks. I'm not hungry."

Micah pulled open the drawer underneath the kitchen sink and gathered up the few tools she kept in her apartment. "Maybe you'll need these," she offered as she placed them on the floor beside Rob.

"I don't think so. It's been so long since I've hooked one of these up, I can't remember exactly how to do this."

Micah sat down, cross-legged on the floor next to him, and read over the operating directions as he worked. "This will be great, Rob. When someone calls, I can hear them talk. Then, if it's important, I can pick up the phone and talk to them."

"And if you hear that Scott's voice again, you can let him talk to the machine," he said in a low tone.

"He won't be calling again," Micah assured him, trying to suppress a grin. A possessive streak was a quality she sometimes liked in a man.

"What I want to know is why he called in the first place." Rob sat the machine rather noisily on the stand by the phone and reached into the box for the cassette tape. "Your relationship with him is obviously over. Isn't he aware of that?"

"I reminded him and told him I'm involved with someone." Micah pushed some of her long curls back over her shoulder and pretended to concentrate on the instruction booklet in her hands. This conversation would be better ended, she knew.

"So that was it? He wasn't any more persistent than to simply say, 'okay'?"

Rob was the one being persistent. Why did he ask

these questions? She knew she would give him an honest answer, and he knew it, too.

"Well, no, he wanted to see me anyway, but—"

"How long has it been since you've dated him?" Rob slid the cassette tape into place and snapped shut the lid. Piercing blue eyes now focused on her, but Micah kept her eyes glued to the operation instructions she still held in her hands.

"I don't know. About a year, I suppose," she answered. "Our breakup is not a date I keep on my calendar."

"Is it over, Micah?" he asked.

She looked up into his frowning face. "I just said we stopped seeing each other over a year—"

"No, I mean the way you felt about him. Is it over?"

"Yes, of course it is," Micah responded quickly. "I told him I was involved with you and that it's…"

Rob studied her wavering green gaze. "Serious." He finished her sentence.

She nodded her head without speaking.

"It is, you know." Rob touched her cheek lightly.

"I know," she agreed in a whisper. "But there are things you don't know about me, Rob. Things—"

"Things that you're ready to tell me?" Rob interrupted. "I'm not going back to that old argument of yours. We're already involved, Micah, and until you're prepared to give me specific reasons why we can't remain together, I'm not going to discuss it."

He turned a couple of dials on the answering machine, and then said, "Here. Record a message to answer the calls."

"Let me think of what I want to say before you turn it on."

"Tell them you can't come to the phone, but you'll return the call as soon as possible. Be sure to tell them to leave their name and number."

"Maybe I should 'ask' them to leave their information," she said in response to his brisk orders.

"Ask them, tell them, whatever. Are you ready?"

She recorded a brief message and when she finished, they played it back.

"Sounds good," Rob commented as he began to rewind the tape.

"Rob..." She touched his hand, bringing his action to a halt. "Thank you...for the answering machine and the ice cream."

"For disrupting your peaceful day with two nephews and a niece in need of a sitter?"

She laughed. "That, too. I really think they had a pretty good time. Don't you?"

"Yes," he answered, sliding over to sit closer to her on the living-room floor. "But it wasn't exactly the day I would have planned for us."

"Me, neither," she responded. "But we'll have other rainy days." She glanced up at the nearby window and saw the rain continue to fall. She scrambled to her feet and opened the window, allowing the cool scent of rain to enter. "Shh." She held her fingers to her lips as she sat down beside Rob again, close to the sofa so they could both lean back against it. She rested her head on his shoulder, and they sat quietly on the floor. "Hear the rain hitting the leaves on the apple tree?" she said.

Rob kissed the top of her head, his mouth moving against her soft hair. "Yes, hon, I hear it."

Micah nestled closer to him. "You couldn't have slept much last night. You didn't leave here until nearly two-thirty this morning, and didn't you say Angela brought the kids at 5:00 a.m.?"

"Uh-huh," he confirmed as Micah turned her head enough to see if his eyes were still open. As she suspected, they were not.

"You'll be more comfortable on the couch," she offered with a gentle nudge to his side. "You need to get some rest."

"No, I—"

"Go on." She patted a sofa cushion behind them. "You're exhausted, Rob. You need to sleep."

"Maybe for a little while," he replied quietly.

Micah disappeared into the bedroom for a moment and returned with a multicolored afghan and tossed it over his sleeping form.

Then she retrieved her easel from the back room and set it up in the living room in front of the window. The church was taking form as the central focus of the painting, but the sky was what she was working on now. The few wispy clouds accented the beautiful blue sky.

A few minute's rest turned into a couple of hours, as Micah had suspected they would. The trial had been demanding, and Rob had looked very tired last night and all day today. Smiling, she continued with her work. She had never imagined herself pleased with a date who fell asleep on her living-room sofa. She must be falling in— She stopped, paintbrush in midair and gazed at the man asleep on her couch. So this was what love was like? Being happy just to have him in the same apartment with her, even sleeping? That, and the way she could feel as though he had touched her with only a gentle look? And when he kissed her...

Rob stirred, and Micah returned her concentration to the canvas.

"What are you doing?" he asked, sitting up slowly and running a hand through his disheveled hair.

"Working," she replied. "I've been trying to finish this painting for weeks."

"What time is it, anyway?" he asked, glancing down at his watch.

"Nine-fifteen."

"Nine-fifteen? I've been asleep nearly two hours. Why didn't you wake me?"

"You were tired. I know you didn't get much rest last night," Micah replied, "and I liked watching you sleep."

He glanced at his watch again. "I've got to get home so I can look over a few notes for tomorrow."

Standing up, he smoothed some wrinkles from his clothes. "Some date, huh? I bring three kids here for you to supervise and feed, and then I fall asleep on your sofa."

"It was rather unique," she said quietly. But it had been a day she enjoyed.

Rob wasn't smiling, but that tenderness in his eyes couldn't be mistaken, and it always made her smile.

"Thank you, Micah, for the help with the kids...for answering your door at two in the morning..."

"You're welcome," she responded. "I could still fix a pizza if you'd like to stay awhile."

"No, I can't. I'll get a sandwich on the way home." He pulled his jacket from the closet.

"How about chocolate ice cream?" she offered, watching him slip into the lightweight, gray jacket. She suspected he disliked leaving as much as she hated letting him go.

"Maybe next time," he replied. The weariness returned to his face as he stood by the door, ready to leave. "I don't know when I'll see you again. Who knows when this nightmare of a trial will end."

"When it does, I'll be here," she answered.

"And so will I," he said and kissed her on the forehead before disappearing into the damp night air.

Micah closed the door and the window, shutting

out the cool evening breeze. Walking to the sofa, she picked up the afghan to fold it into a neat square and return it to the closet, but the faint smell of his cologne lingered on it, bringing her action to a halt. Hugging it to her frame, the warmth brought tears to her eyes.

"Oh, Rob," she whispered. Then she sank into the cushions, enjoying the warmth of his napping place. "What am I going to do with you?"

Chapter Eight

Monday and Tuesday passed with no word from Rob, but they were beautiful, happy days for Micah because she knew she would see him again. They would have more times together, once the trial ended.

When she entered her apartment on Wednesday evening, Patches followed her through the front door into her living room, where Micah found the red light flashing on her answering machine. She pushed the play button.

"Hi, Micah. This is your beautician, otherwise known as your best friend, Carole. It's good that you've patched things up with Rob, but don't forget you have other friends, other responsibilities. Call me sometime and, as the saying goes, 'We'll do lunch.'"

The beep sounded, and another message began.

"Hello. Glad you're using the answering machine. It's seven forty-eight, Wednesday morning." She smiled at his preciseness. "I didn't expect you to leave for school so early. The trial should be over in a day or two. Things are looking up. I'll let you know what happens. Bye." Then a pause. "I miss you."

"I miss you, too," she whispered, placing a hand on the recorder.

The third and fourth calls were from salesmen suggesting she buy aluminum siding.

"For an apartment I rent? I don't think so," she murmured, then rewound the tape and clicked off the machine.

"C'mon, kitty," Micah called her furry companion to the front door. "Mrs. Poe will wonder where you've disappeared to," she said, watching the cat scamper through the open doorway.

The clock showed a few minutes after six, so she turned on the television. The news, already in progress, showed an older, white-haired gentleman being interviewed as he stood on the courthouse steps. The face was not familiar, but the name that the reporter mentioned caught Micah's attention. Alsmore. Attorney Taylor Alsmore was the man on the screen. She turned up the volume to hear his words while he beamed about a victorious verdict in the murder trial that had concluded earlier that afternoon. Micah sat on the corner of the heavy old coffee table, never moving her eyes from the picture as Alsmore glowed and raved about justice...about simply doing his job...and about the appropriateness of jury trials. Micah's mouth dropped open in surprise. The Gendersen trial had been in the news for the past two weeks, but Micah skipped over the articles and newscasts. She had followed one trial, word for word, years ago, and had determined never to do that again. But Rob had not mentioned that this was the trial he was so busy with. A murder trial. Of course, she could have taken more of an interest, asked more questions about his work. Micah turned off the television and stood staring into the darkening screen. Law, trials, courtrooms, attorneys. Why had she fallen in love with someone who was so involved in all of that?

Through her sandwich and potato chips and later through a hurried shower, she waited for his call. But it didn't come. By ten o'clock, she was in bed with a book in her hands that was quickly laid aside at the first ring of the telephone.

"Congratulations! You won," Micah said as soon as she heard Rob's familiar hello.

"Thanks. You never know how things are going to turn out with a jury," he replied.

"You didn't tell me it was the Gendersen trial, a murder case."

"I don't usually want to discuss work when I'm with you, Micah."

She smiled, and then tucking stray hair behind her

ear, she asked, "Did you see the news? Did you see Alsmore taking all the credit?"

"Alsmore is good at that. And he *is* the senior partner, you know."

"But, Rob, it's not fair for him to get all the glory. How can you stand—"

"Honey, if I got upset about everything in this firm that I didn't agree with, I wouldn't be a very pleasant person to be around," Rob replied. "Tell me how your day was."

"My day? It was okay, but it couldn't compare to yours."

He laughed. "I thought you didn't like courtroom drama?"

"I don't," she answered gently, "but I'm proud of you. You should feel good about what you've done."

"What I'd feel good about is seeing you. What are you doing?"

"I'm in bed, reading," she responded.

Rob remained quiet for a moment, and Micah had the intuitive feeling that he had decided against saying whatever had crossed his mind.

"Tomorrow night?" he asked.

"Tomorrow is Thursday. I'm teaching two classes in the evening. How about Friday?"

"Friday? Is that the best we can do?"

"I'm afraid so. That is, unless you want to come over now for a while," she offered.

He hesitated. "No, it's late, and I don't want to keep you from a good book."

"It's not *that* good," she answered, laughing softly.

"I'm sorry I couldn't call earlier, Micah, but I had clients waiting for me when I got back to the office."

"You've been working too much," she said out of what she knew to be selfish motives. She had wanted to be with him this evening and even now, to see him, talk to him, touch him. "Maybe you should have told them to come back tomorrow."

"I wanted to." The answer sounded firm, resolute. And Rob's voice sounded tired. "But their fifteen-year-old son had been picked up for breaking and entering. This family has three kids, all boys. The oldest one is the problem now, but the other two are headed down the same path soon."

"Is there any way to help them?"

"I don't know, Micah. I'll do what I can with legal help, but what they need is some family counseling. And God. How could anyone expect to raise three children in today's world without God in their lives?"

Micah opened her mouth to respond but found herself speechless. She could hardly believe what she was hearing. Rob offering the Lord as a solution?

"I called Brian Andrews over at Third Avenue

Church. They just finished a building project over there, and they have a new gym."

"I've heard about that," she acknowledged quickly. Micah's heart soared with possibilities. She had always believed Rob would one day find his way back to God, but this was the best sign she'd seen yet.

"Brian is the youth pastor there. He was in that teen group I belonged to years ago. He said they have some open nights at the gym, and they're starting to organize basketball games. Maybe I can get this kid interested in something that will keep him out of trouble."

"Did he agree to go?"

"If I go with him," Rob answered. "And since you're busy tomorrow, I guess I'll be picking him up, by myself, at six o'clock."

Micah chose her words carefully. "That's a start," she said. For the teen and Rob, she considered. "Who knows? Maybe it will be fun."

"Right." Rob's tone was filled with skepticism. "I don't know how I get into these situations."

"You're compassionate and very decisive," Micah commented. "You see something that needs to be done, and you do it."

"Right," he growled. "And my impetuous tendencies get me into situations that I later regret."

"You won't regret this, Rob. It could change this boy's life." And Rob's, Micah added silently to herself. If only he'd let it. "See you Friday?"

"I'll be there at six."

"I'll be waiting," she responded, and there was silence between them.

"I miss you." The gentleness in his voice brought a lump to her throat.

"Friday?" she repeated.

"Friday," he replied quietly. "Good night, Micah."

"Good night," she said in a voice barely above a whisper. Closing the daily devotional book close at hand, she placed it on the floor beneath her bed and turned off the light. Friday seemed as far away as Rob did at that moment.

The hours at school the next morning seemed to drag by, and Micah needed something to break up the long stretch of time standing between her and Rob.

"I'm using my lunch period and break time to go downtown and pick up some supplies I need for class this afternoon," Micah explained to Angela while preparing to exit the building. "I'll be back in less than an hour."

That sunny Thursday afternoon was a lovely day in late April made even lovelier by the fact that her old station wagon started on the first try. It had given her very little trouble lately. Everything looked and felt wonderfully, beautifully right for once in her life.

She drove the short distance to the art supply store

in town and ran inside to pick up the craft sticks, poster board and other supplies she had ordered. Much more quickly than she had anticipated, she headed back in the direction of the school. Back to papers to grade, kids to control and more hours of waiting. The thirty extra minutes before her next class were like a breath of fresh air, but the hours until Friday seemed endless. She decided to surprise Rob with a visit.

Soon she pulled into the parking lot behind Alsmore, Barlett and Maine's office building. Rob would probably be at lunch. Her watch showed a quarter past twelve, but she would take the chance.

A trio of secretaries exited the building as Micah neared the front door. All were tall, willowy young women whom Micah eyed curiously. A blonde, a brunette and a redhead. Not the soft auburn of her own curly hair, Micah noticed, but a brassy red. Did they work with Rob? She had only been in his office once, and she couldn't recall seeing any of them.

"Hello. May I help you?" asked the friendly, pert young woman at the receptionist's desk as Micah entered the cool, air-conditioned suite of offices.

"Is Rob Granston in?" Maybe she had made a mistake in coming. What had seemed a good idea a few minutes ago, now felt like an intrusion.

"Yes, I believe he's still here. Your name, please?"

"Micah Shepherd."

The receptionist disappeared into the office Micah

remembered entering the last time she had been here. Soon the woman reappeared in the doorway. "You can go right in, Miss Shepherd."

Micah stepped past the young lady into Rob's office, and the door clicked shut.

"Hello, Miss Shepherd," Rob said as he rose from his chair and walked around the corner of his desk, his mouth slanting into a smile.

Her heart quickened its pace when he approached her, touching her only with his warm gaze. "Good afternoon," she answered.

"You need to speak with an attorney?" The question was lightly stated, almost taunting, and his eyes flashed with amusement.

"With one in particular," she replied in her most professional tone.

"And what is it you wish to speak with me about?" he asked, leaning near her and grazing her earlobe with a light, teasing kiss.

The faint aroma of his cologne filled her senses, and her desire to see him increased quickly to the need to touch. And so she did. First his shirt and then his tie, her fingers gliding along the edge, straightening it. She looked up at him through long, dark lashes. "Speaking isn't exactly what I had in mind," she said softly, and rising on her tiptoe, she invited his kiss—a slow, tender meeting that clouded her thoughts and warmed her heart and soul. Micah's arms slid around his neck, her fingers weaving into soft, black hair, straight and fine. As Rob's hands moved against her back, pulling her close, Micah could feel the hammering of his heart against her own, and the kiss went on and on until—

A buzzer rang, shattering the moment, and the receptionist's voice came over the intercom advising Rob of a call.

Micah buried her face in his shirt, muffling a laugh. But Rob was not laughing. He muttered something undistinguishable while reaching for the telephone on the desk beside them. "Take a message, Jackie. I'll return the call later."

"But Mr. Alsmore wants you. He needs to review the Holcomb case with you. Could you take the file and meet him in his office in fifteen minutes?"

Micah raised a hand to her mouth to cover the light laughter. She turned away from Rob while he agreed to meet with his boss, then instructed the receptionist to hold his calls. Micah stood glancing over the framed diplomas displayed on one wall of Rob's office until he finished.

"Thank you, Jackie," Rob concluded and glanced briefly through several manila folders stacked on his desk.

"Rob...this diploma...it's from Trinity," Micah said.

"Uh-huh," he confirmed without looking up. "Where did I put that Holcomb file?"

"You did your undergraduate work at a Christian college? Why didn't you tell me?"

"It didn't seem important enough to mention.

Here it is,'' he commented, pulling out the folder he needed.

"It's important to me. I knew you were a Christian, but for how long?"

"Ten years." Rob placed the Holcomb file on his chair. "Now, can we get back to what we were doing before we were so rudely interrupted?" He moved closer to Micah again, taking her in his arms easily, naturally.

"That's a long time, Rob. And after ten years, Nick died and that was it? You just stopped going to church? Stopped believing?"

"I think you're familiar with the term 'backslide'?"

"But, Rob—"

He placed an index finger gently against her lips to silence her. "I believed for a while, and then, one day, I didn't." Rob lowered his hand from her mouth to clasp her hand warmly in his own. Then he lightly kissed her frown. "You said you didn't come here to talk. Remember?"

"She can't hear us, can she?" Micah asked as she looked toward the intercom. "I mean, I thought we were alone, and then she started speaking."

"We're alone," he responded, "until you pick up the phone or someone opens the door."

Micah slipped away, moving only inches from him, and adjusted her rumpled skirt and blouse. "It seems so funny, being in your office, kissing like that with people just outside the door.'' She motioned toward the entrance she had come through.

Rob touched her face gently as a trace of a smile crossed his lips. ''It didn't seem funny to me, but maybe if we try again—''

''Someone might walk in,'' she protested, but did not move away from his touch.

''Not without knocking, they won't. Common courtesy, Micah.''

''Common courtesy or a master plan devised to prevent interruptions of such displays of affection?'' Micah teased. ''Tell me, Counselor, are you accustomed to this type of behavior in this office?''

''Absolutely,'' he responded. ''It's an everyday occurrence.''

''Rob!'' Micah punched him playfully in the arm. The joking had gone far enough. She had seen too many attractive women in this building.

''Worried, huh?'' he said quietly, drawing her back into his warm embrace. ''Is that why you came down here today? To check on me?''

''No, I...I really only meant to stop in and say hi.''

His hand touched the soft skin under her chin, tilting her gaze up to his. ''Hi,'' he offered in a deadly calm voice, and his darkening eyes searched her face. ''Satisfied?''

Micah stared into compelling blue, fighting the urge to shake her head no. Snatches of time and a few promising kisses would never—

"Me, neither," he responded.

"I...I have to get back," she said, stumbling through her statement. This was an office, a place of business, and there were people only a few feet away on the other side of the door. Micah felt as if they could somehow be seen through that irritating intercom. "I have to get back to school. My next class is due to start soon."

"All right," he conceded. Or did he? The firm hands sliding up her arms seemed to have no intention of letting her go. "Goodbye," Rob said in an almost casual tone, but there was nothing casual in the reaction between them when their mouths met again in a kiss that was tender only in its beginning. They both needed, wanted more than a few moments together offered.

"Rob," she breathed his name as the draining kiss came to a slow, almost painful end. "I've got to leave."

He released her, reluctance in every movement.

"Tomorrow night?" she whispered softly, needlessly.

"I'll be there. Six o'clock," he replied as she turned from him. "Micah, before you go...my parents are having a dinner this Sunday. One o'clock. Liz and my brother and their families will be there. They'd like you to come."

Meeting his family. She cringed at the thought. There had been no involvement, no relationship for her serious enough to warrant meeting the family since California. She blinked. It had been a very long time. "Rob..."

"*I* want you to come," he added with emphasis.

A soft sigh escaped. Micah had survived an encounter with one irate, accusatory mom. Maybe it was time to take another chance. "If it's important to you," she said.

"It is," he responded, obviously pleased with her answer. "I'll walk you to your car."

"No, really. That's not necessary. I'll see you tomorrow." Touching her lips to the palm of her hand, she blew a kiss across the room before she slipped through the doorway.

"No, it *can't* be," Micah protested audibly with the other moviegoers in the midst of laughing at her own inaccuracy when the guilty party was revealed.

"A murder mystery," Rob said dryly. "How did I let you talk me into this after weeks of the Gendersen trial?"

"It was good, didn't you think? I had no idea who the killer was."

"I told you it wasn't the burglar. Too obvious," Rob insisted as they exited the theater, leaving the aroma of buttery popcorn behind for the refreshing spring air.

"I know, I know," Micah responded, still laughing at the surprise ending. "You told me so."

A crooked smile or smirk, Micah couldn't decide which, curved Rob's mouth. "The chauffeur," he said. "I said all along to keep your eye on the innocent-looking driver." He reached down to take her hand in his own, and she was almost startled by the contact. He had not intentionally touched her all evening. Not at her apartment when he first arrived, not during dinner, not once throughout the entire movie.

Micah held tightly to his hand as they walked toward the parking lot. He released her to open the car door. She hated ending the contact, and a quick glance in his direction said as much, but if he could read the feelings in her clear green gaze, he gave no indication.

The film became the topic of conversation on the drive to her apartment—the movie, the lovely spring weather, Micah's classes, Rob's evening out with the troubled teenager he had told her about, and even some discussion about the Gendersen trial.

"So, you had a good time with the pastor, Brian Andrews, and the boy you took to play basketball with him at Third Avenue Church?"

"Yes. Ronnie is the kid's name. Really, it went much better than I thought it would. Ronnie enjoyed himself and wants to go back and take his younger brothers. Brian is picking up the boys on Monday for another game, then I'll take them there again next Thursday."

"That sounds great. Maybe this will make a difference in Ronnie's life."

"It might," he answered. "I think the boy might

be as sick of his lifestyle as his parents and the judicial system are. This could turn him around.'' Rob parked in the familiar slot in front of Mrs. Poe's house. ''You're studying me rather intently,'' he commented.

''I'm keeping my eye on the chauffeur. 'The innocent-looking driver,' as I think you referred to him.''

''I don't have a chauffeur's license, I'm not innocent-looking,'' Rob said, switching off the engine and pulling the keys from the ignition to dangle them in front of Micah. ''And, I am no longer driving.''

''But you are good at spotting the guilty party. Maybe you should be a detective instead of an attorney,'' she suggested.

Rob's smile faded; the slant of his mouth thinned into a straight line.

She had said something wrong, she knew it. But the words should have bothered her more than him. ''What's wrong?'' she asked. ''I was only teasing.''

''Explain something to me, Micah. How could you possibly enjoy watching a murder mystery when the very mention of courtrooms and trials usually sends you into a panic. Were you trying to prove something to me?''

The proof had been for herself. No one else. She could lose herself in the moment of the mystery without looking back. It was the characters' story.

It was their mystery, their crimes, not hers. Just as her father's had been.

"Micah?"

"There was no judge, no jury in that movie. It was about a murder. A whodunit. Not a courtroom drama," she answered defensively. "And I do discuss your work with you. Didn't we talk about the Gendersen trial on the way home? Haven't we—"

"You know what I'm referring to," he interrupted. "Sometimes I can see it in your eyes. The conversation goes the wrong way and—"

"I don't like courtrooms, trials...is that so unusual?" she snapped. "One experience with them was enough, wasn't it? I was just a kid, Rob. It frightened me."

"What frightened you?"

"Everything," she responded, her voice unsteady. "The courtroom was huge and the accusations... there were so many things said—"

"Accusations about what?"

Her mind had gone back nine, no, ten years to the worst part of California: her memories of it.

"Micah—"

"The attorneys, the prosecutors, they were cruel and...relentless. They never let up."

"And so you blame all attorneys for what happened?"

"No, I don't. My mother was an attorney, and I loved her, and there's you..." She looked into his piercing blue gaze. Yes, there was Rob. And there were risks and consequences and far more details that she wanted to disclose.

"I didn't know your mother was dead," he stated when she failed to complete her sentence.

Micah frowned. "She's not. I didn't say she was."

"You said 'loved.' Past tense," he remarked.

"I did?" Micah responded. "No, she's alive... and I do love her. The question is, does she love me?"

Rob's hands rested on the steering wheel, and he looked out into the darkness of the night. "Why would you doubt your mother's love? Was she on trial, too, or was it just your dad?"

"My father." Her voice trembled. "He stole money, embezzled it from the company he'd spent his career with." Micah pulled the door handle to let herself out of the car. "He went to jail, Rob. Can you see how wrong I am for you? If you cared for me, you'd leave this alone." She slammed the door shut behind her.

"Micah." He was out of the automobile and, catching up with her in a few long strides, he gripped her shoulder. "I do care," he said as he turned her around to face him.

"Please, Rob, let me go." She struggled to escape his grasp, but the attempt was futile.

"I do care about you," he said, "and nothing that has happened in the past will change that. But I want to know, Micah. I want to understand."

"You can't understand. Unless you've lived it, you can't know what it's like." She stopped perfectly still, and with pleading eyes she looked into the stormy depths of his gaze. "Please, Rob..."

And Rob released her, waving a hand through the black night air in an empty gesture. "You trust me with today, but not with yesterday. Is that it?"

"I didn't move thousands of miles to go on living in the shadows. If I wanted my past to be a part of my everyday life, I would have stayed in California. But I'm not there, I'm here, with you." She paused. "And this is where I want to be...for now. Don't ask for more."

Rob touched the soft cascade of hair that hung freely around her shoulders, and some of the warmth returned to his eyes. "But I want more...so much more."

There was a noise, a whimper a few feet away from them and Micah turned, her gaze falling on the crumpled ball of fur near the gutter.

"Patches!" She rushed to the curb, kneeling in the grass. "Oh, Rob, it's Patches! Poor baby," she said in a soothing voice as she reached out toward the animal. "She's Mrs. Poe's pet. My landlady."

Rob knelt on one knee beside her as Micah stroked the cat's ears. But there was little response. He placed a hand gently against Patches's matted fur. "Looks pretty bad, Micah."

"Poor dumb kitty. Why couldn't you stay out of the street?" she whispered as though the cat could understand her, and she stroked its forehead as she had done countless times over the past two years. Tears welled up in Micah's eyes. "Mrs. Poe is away for the weekend. We'll have to find a vet." She gathered up the little furry bundle and held Patches close.

"That's not going to be easy this late."

"We have to, Rob. Maybe she'll have to be put to sleep if she's suffering." Then she thought of something. "Dr. Tackett! He lives two streets over. We can take her over there."

"Honey—"

"Please, Rob. Maybe he can do something."

Without saying another word, Rob opened the passenger door of his car and Micah climbed into the front seat.

"There's a towel that I use for my paintings in the back seat of my station wagon. Pull the back door open, and you'll find it," Micah explained, and he followed her instructions. Within seconds, he was handing her the towel, expecting her to place it across her legs beneath the cat, but instead she covered Patches with it.

A short while later, they approached the veterinarian's street. "There it is. The third house on the right," Micah said, pointing to Dr. Tackett's home.

"Yes?" the white-haired gentleman asked, opening the door after their first knock.

"Dr. Tackett, I'm Micah Shepherd. One of Mrs.

Poe's tenants from Spring Blossom Avenue. This is Patches, Mrs. Poe's pet, and——''

''Well, mercy sakes, I remember Patches. Come here, kitty.'' He pulled back the towel to see the bundle in Micah's arms.

''We're not sure what happened,'' Rob stated after they had stepped inside the doctor's home. ''We just found her.''

''Well, let's have a look-see at your little friend.''

They followed the man into a small office off to the side of the hallway they had entered, and Micah placed Patches, still wrapped in the towel, on the table. The doctor went about his work while Rob moved to stand behind Micah, gently placing his hands on her shoulders.

''This looks serious, kids. I'm not so sure she's going to pull through,'' the vet said when he looked up at them. ''Leave her here with me.''

Micah agreed to do that, and Rob squeezed her shoulders a little before releasing her. He pulled a business card from his wallet and handed it to the doctor. ''Here's my name and address. You can send the bill to me at my office. We appreciate your time, Dr. Tackett.''

''But, where's Mrs. Poe? This is her pet, isn't it? She——''

''She's away for the night visiting her sister. She'll be back in the morning. I'll ask her to call you then,'' Micah explained, wiping away a tear with the back of her hand.

"The best thing to do is leave Patches here with me," the doctor stated, showing them to the door.

They thanked the man again for his help and walked to Rob's car in silence to make the short trip back to Micah's apartment.

The glare of the porch light hurt Micah's eyes, and she turned away from it, jiggling her purse in search of her keys. "Here they are," she said finally and soon her key turned in the lock. She opened the door and they stood in the entryway for a while. "I'm sorry for being such a crybaby."

"It's okay," he said quietly as he took her into his arms. Micah placed her head against his chest, listening to the steady beat of his heart. "Do you want me to talk to Mrs. Poe for you?"

"No," she replied with a sniff. "I'll tell her when she gets home."

Rob held her close, and there was nothing Micah knew that was as comforting as being in his arms.

"Thank you for offering to pay, but that's Mrs. Poe's responsibility."

"Forget about it. It doesn't matter," he answered, searching her face when she raised her head to look up at him. "You okay?"

"Yes," she responded and cleared her throat. "It's just that…oh, Rob, I love that stupid cat," she cried before burying her face in the soft material of his shirt.

"I know," he said quietly. "I know you do." He held her close while she cried, and only after she had completely quieted in his arms, did he speak again. "Will you be all right when I leave?"

"Yes," she replied, reaching for a tissue on the end table nearby.

"I think you should get some sleep." Rob kissed the top of her head. "You'll feel better in the morning."

Micah looked up at him and wiped her nose with the tissue. This was not how she had thought this evening would end.

"I'll call you," he told her and opened the door.

"Okay," she responded. "Good night, Rob."

"Good night." He smiled and left.

Micah fastened the dead-bolt lock on her front door and switched on another light in the living room. Walking past the full-length mirror that hung in the hallway, she stopped abruptly, startled by her own reflection. The colorful skirt she'd worn tonight was now marred, the green blouse, sprinkled with cat hair and blood, and a trickle of mascara trailed down the side of her face. She pulled another tissue from the box and wiped away the smeared eye makeup.

"Silly cat," she murmured as she walked into the kitchen. "Why did you have to play in the traffic, anyway?" Walking to the table, she saw a note sticking out from beneath the saltshaker. Realizing Carole must have used the apartment key Micah had given to her in case of emergency, she picked up the slip of paper and began to read Carole's haphazard scribbling:

> Hi!
> Used your key—emergency! Date with a cute accountant I told you about and no shoes to match my new skirt. I borrowed your red ones. Thanks!
>
> Luv ya,
Carole
>
> P.S. I brought in your mail. Who do you know in Paris?

The note fell from Micah's hand and floated down to the table while she turned to the hutch. The mail. There it was. Micah pushed a charge-card statement and some advertisements to the side and picked up the letter from France. Tears slid down her cheeks, blurring the ink as they plopped, one by one, onto the envelope.

Getting into his automobile, Rob leaned over to pick up a piece of the frayed, old towel Micah had placed over Patches. Rob held the small scrap of terry cloth in his hand and thought of the woman to whom he had just said good-night. Grass and blood stained the front of Micah's floral print skirt, stains from kneeling to comfort Patches. Tears over a cat, a cat that wasn't even hers. Rob shook his head, his fingers closing tightly around the piece of cloth. Micah's watery green eyes remained in his memory as he silently sat there. Her eyes and those crumpled, stained clothes that she had not seemed to even notice. Tossing the cloth onto the floorboard, he clasped the steering wheel firmly in his hands. He had known it before now, but he had not felt it as sharply as he did tonight when he'd knelt beside her in the grass, seeing her tenderness. He loved her. The gentle-natured, auburn-haired young woman who painted pictures and cried over other people's pets. The love was there as none had ever been before. Sharp, painful, wonderful, real. He should have told her before tonight. Should he tell her now?

Rob started the car engine and pulled away from the curb. He would find another time to tell her. There would be a better time. There had to be.

Chapter Nine

❧

Telling Mrs. Poe proved easier than Micah had supposed. Patches ran out into the street too often, according to her owner. She'd always known it would happen one day. A call to Dr. Tackett confirmed the worst. Patches was gone.

Micah went back to her apartment angry at Mrs. Poe for her callousness, angry at the letter from her mother, angry at how much she now wanted a man she couldn't have. After putting on jeans and a T-shirt and pulling her hair up into a ponytail, she headed for the small flower bed just outside her back door. Working up the soil for the impatiens she would plant soon seemed like a good idea. She heard the ringing of the phone while reaching for a shovel and the click of the answering machine as it recorded Rob's message. But it was a nearby voice that caused her to look up from her gardening.

"Hey, Micah! How ya doin'?" Carole called as she walked up the brick path toward her.

"Hi," she answered, brushing some stray hair from the side of her face. "What's up?"

"I've brought back your shoes. I hope you don't mind my borrowing them without asking."

"I don't mind." Micah went back to the digging, turning the dirt over a shovelful at a time.

"Aren't you going to ask me how my date was?" Carole inquired. She placed the shoes on the back step.

No, Micah hadn't planned to ask. Someone else's happy love life might be more than she could bear this morning. But Carole would be hurt. "Nice guy?" was all she could manage.

"Nice and handsome and—" Carole stopped. "Did you go out with Rob last night?"

"Yes. To dinner and a movie."

"And then?" Carole persisted while watching Micah work.

"And we came home and found Patches lying in the gutter. Hit by a car, I guess."

"Oh, I'm sorry. Is she okay?"

"No." Micah leaned the shovel against the wall. "She's dead."

"I really am sorry," Carole responded. "I kind of liked that little feline."

"Yeah, me, too," Micah answered quietly.

"Is there anything I can do to help?" Carole asked.

"No," Micah said sadly. "I'm afraid not."

"Well, okay, I'll leave you alone. When you're feeling better, call me and I'll buy us a pizza."

Micah smiled. "Okay."

"By the way, who do you know in France? Do you have a secret admirer hidden away somewhere that you've forgotten to mention to me?"

"No," she replied and wiped her hands on her old jeans. "That letter was from my mother."

"Your mother? The one you *never* hear from? The one you won't talk about?"

"The only one I have," Micah answered.

"You've never told me she lives in France."

"She has for a long time."

"So, what did she say? I mean, you don't have to tell me, but what did she want? After all this time?"

"Nothing, really."

"I know. You don't want to talk about it. So, what else is new?"

"She wants the same things she always wants— to know I'm okay, that I'm not making mistakes with my life. Helpful hints from Mom," she stated, her voice sharpened in sarcasm. She sighed. "I'm not up to this today, Carole. Could we talk later?"

"Micah, maybe I tease you and question you too much, but you're one of the best friends I've ever had," Carole said, shielding her eyes from the sunlight with an uplifted hand. "It doesn't have to be me, but you need to talk to someone about this.

There's a lot of unfinished business between you and your parents that you need to deal with.''

"I know," Micah replied. "But today...I just can't.''

Carole reached out, squeezing Micah's arm affectionately. "Call me.''

Micah assured her friend she would, then watched her walk past the shrubbery then down the same path that had brought her there. Then it was back to the dirt, the weeds and the empty flower bed waiting to be filled with colorful offerings.

"Lord, I'm sorry," she said softly. "Sorry I'm so angry with my mother, and sorry I disappointed her. And sorry I'll disappoint Rob," she added as she carefully set some impatiens into the ground, covering their roots with topsoil. "And I'm sorry I miss Dad so much. If I could just talk to him....'' But she wouldn't, she knew. It was not what he wanted.

It was past lunchtime and Micah's stomach growled, reminding her that last night's beef Stroganoff was long gone. Breakfast hadn't sounded appealing at all. Even a simple glass of milk brought thoughts of Patches.

The phone rang again. Micah kicked off her dirty tennis shoes and hurried into the apartment barefoot. It would be Rob. And he would call until she answered.

"Hello.''

"Hi," Rob said quietly and then paused. "Have you spoken to Mrs. Poe yet?''

"Yes, and she called Dr. Tackett. Patches is gone."

"Sorry," he responded gently. "Did she take it hard?"

"Not as hard as I did." Micah's soft laugh followed her reply.

"But that probably made it worse for you."

"I'll get over it. I shouldn't be so sensitive, I guess."

Rob's response was quick and comforting. "I like you just the way you are. Don't find fault in yourself over this."

"No, I suppose I shouldn't. It's just...I got a letter from my mother in yesterday's mail. She has a way of doing that to me."

He didn't respond right away, then, "The letter, was it bad news?"

"No, nothing new, really. Same old stuff...family stuff. Rob, do you think we ever get out from under it?"

"All families are different, so I can't comment about yours. But, with mine, some things never improve. You know? It's kind of like my mother's fruitcake at Christmas. It's really bad, but we eat it anyway to keep her happy. 'Blessed are the peacemakers,' as they say."

"Hmm, I distinctly remember reading that in the New Testament. I thought you didn't have any interest in that way of thinking anymore."

"That's true, I don't. But, unfortunately, I have a

great memory, and some things I've learned won't be forgotten. No matter how hard I try.''

"I guess it's that way with some things." She hesitated. "But with my family, well, our problems don't stem from home-baked desserts." She gave a sad, soft laugh. "I wish they did.''

"So do I,'' was Rob's immediate reply. "Micah, I get the feeling that your situation is serious enough that we shouldn't be joking about it at all.''

"But laughing feels much better than crying,'' she told him. "And I certainly don't feel like crying, so let's talk about something else. Your parents' dinner tomorrow. Am I going to have to eat fruitcake?''

"No, not until December,'' Rob assured her with a laugh. "My folks are looking forward to meeting you.''

"I'm so nervous about this—''

"Don't be. They're friendly, common people, Micah. You'll like them. And as I told you, Liz and the kids will be there, too, so that will help you feel more at ease.''

"What time will you pick me up?'' she asked.

"Dinner is at one o'clock. What time do you usually get home from church?''

"Around noon. You could come to church with me, you know.''

"Thanks. I'll pass on that offer, but I'll meet you at your place at noon. I've got to get caught up on some work at the office today. How about this evening? Are you free?''

"No, and I know this sounds ridiculous on a Saturday night, but I'm going to a student's home to do some tutoring. He's missed a lot of school this year, and I'm trying to help him catch up before the year ends." She exhaled audibly in frustration. "Sorry. I'd much rather be with you," she admitted.

"Me, too," Rob responded. "Well, tell this kid I'm jealous of him, even if he's only in elementary school. He's taking you away from me on a Saturday evening."

"Thank you for being jealous," she said with a smile. "I'll see you tomorrow."

"See you then," he answered and hung up.

Their conversation ended without Micah saying any of the things she needed to say. Agreeing to meet Rob's family was so unlike her that she could hardly believe she had said she would. Maybe it wasn't only her heart she was losing to this man. Maybe her common sense was going, too. She punched in the numbers to Carole's apartment.

"I'm sorry I am unable to answer the phone now. At the sound of the beep, you know what to do," was played back in Carole's recorded voice. Micah almost hung up, then decided to leave a short message.

"Carole, call me when you get home. I—"

Then a shrill beep cut off Micah's words and the answering machine.

"I'm here, Micah. Hang on a second." Then another beeping tone. "Okay, it's off. Sorry about that, but I just walked in the door. Hey, you wanna go get that pizza?''

"How did you know?" Micah asked.

"Lucky guess. Meet me at Baacardi's in, say, fifteen minutes?"

"I'll be there" came the answer, and in less than half an hour, the two women were seated in a booth at a crowded pizza shop enjoying their lunch while a younger generation played video games all around them.

"So, you talked to Rob and now you feel better?" Carole inquired. "You sure didn't feel like doing this an hour ago."

"No, I talked to Rob and now I feel worse. That's where you come into the picture," Micah explained, taking a sip of her root beer. "I'm meeting his family tomorrow. We're going to his parents' home for dinner."

"Wow. That sound's promising. There could be a diamond ring in this somewhere."

"I don't want a diamond ring."

"So tell him you prefer sapphires. He'll understand."

"No, I mean, I can't marry him, so I can't become engaged to him…so I shouldn't be dating him. So, why am I meeting his family?"

Carole studied the frustration apparent in Micah's confused expression without responding.

"Carole, explain this to me. Am I losing my mind?"

"Maybe," Carole replied. "Or maybe you're in love, really in love for the first time in your life. And maybe you want to see how it feels to be part of a big, happy family, his family, even if it's for only one day."

Micah nodded her head in acknowledgment. "And I'm setting us up for heartache."

"You and Rob both. But you must go tomorrow. As long as you're still seeing him, there's still that chance that you'll find a way to make it work."

"I've tried to work this out in my mind a million times, but I can't see a way around it."

"Have you discussed it with Rob? I mean, everything about your family, your fears...everything?"

"No, not completely, but—"

"This doesn't have anything to do with a promise you made to God, or anything like that, does it? I recall hearing you say, in the past, that you thought you might be a minister's wife someday. You didn't make some secret commitment—"

"No, no, of course not," Micah answered. "It has nothing to do with that. I haven't even thought of a future with anyone else since Rob came into my life."

"Well, you must go tomorrow. You've told him you would. And, if you go and enjoy it, you'll be that much more determined to make it work, no matter what your mom writes in those letters from France. I swear, Micah, how could your parents be so far away and, yet, so controlling? Don't let them tell you what you can and cannot do. They don't know Rob. For goodness' sake, they don't even know you anymore, if, in fact, they *ever* really did at all.''

"Okay, so, I'll go. I told him I would.''

"That's right. You have to do this. And then you have to let me know what happens. That's my charge for this brief consultation of ours today. Details.''

"Right,'' Micah responded with a smile. "I should've known this advice wasn't free.''

"Hey, what—''

Micah raised a hand to Carole's mouth. "I know, I know! 'What are friends for?''' she finished Carole's statement. "Let's eat this pizza before it's too cold to enjoy.''

"Great idea,'' Carole remarked, and they finished their meal together before going their separate ways.

When Micah returned to her apartment, there was only one thing left to do, and she wondered why the best thing she could do, ironically, so often became the last resort. She pulled her white Bible from the bookcase and knelt beside her bed without even opening the leather-bound treasure in her hands. Micah owned several different Bibles and kept all of them in the top of her bookcase, even this old favorite. It had belonged to a grandmother, but Micah's father had her name engraved on the cover and passed it on to her since he had little interest in religious matters and, therefore, had no real use of it. And it hadn't meant all that much to Micah until it became nearly all that remained. The Bible, her locket and a suitcase full of clothes.

"Lord, I've come through so much, and you've always been there—everywhere—with me. Even when I wasn't aware of your presence. And you've guided me—if not directly, then indirectly, through the hands of others. Help me now. Give me the wisdom to know what to do and the strength to do it. And Rob...you know, I love him, Lord. These feelings...I can't believe they're not from you. And the things that will tear us apart aren't our fault. It just feels unfair, so unfair." Letting her Bible slip from her hands, Micah buried her face in the bedspread and wept...for all that would never be. When she quieted in the stillness of her bedroom, she reached for a tissue on the night stand. "Now I sound like Rob, don't I? Telling you what's fair and what's not. Just like Nick and Rachel's deaths, Lord. We'll never understand things like that, but Rob needs to have faith in you anyway. Maybe that's the only reason you allowed us to meet...so I could somehow help him come back to you. Show him the way, Lord. Let him know you can be trusted, that you're still working in his life even in the midst of things we don't understand. And either show me some way that will allow us to be together, or show me when, and how, to let him go...." "To let him go." That phrase ran over and over in Micah's mind. How would she ever let him go?

* * *

When Sunday noon finally arrived, Micah was growing increasingly anxious about the visit. Rob picked her up right after church as he had said he would, and he told her how lovely she looked in the orange-red print dress she wore. And Micah did not tell him it was her final choice after having tried on a dozen others.

"Oh, Rob, why did I agree to this? I'm so nervous—"

But it was too late to back out then, as Rob pulled into the driveway of the home where he had grown up. It was an average-looking split-level home, large enough for three, maybe four, bedrooms, with an attached two-car garage. The Granston house was nice, but nothing like the huge house of Micah's childhood. Nothing like it in more ways than appearance, too, Micah suspected. Unpleasant thoughts creased her forehead with a frown.

Rob leaned over and kissed her on the temple. "You will have a good time. Trust me."

And she did trust him. More than anyone else she'd known in all her life. They exited the car and she took his hand as they headed up the walkway.

Rob's parents opened the front door before Rob and Micah had reached the top step. It reminded Micah, for an instant, of the prodigal son's father, waiting and watching for his boy to return.

"We're so glad you could come, dear," stated Rob's mom as she went to Micah, not Rob, for the first hug. Micah smiled nervously and thanked her for the invitation.

"As you've already figured out, this is Micah." Rob made the needless introductions. "And, Micah, these are my parents, Ed and Grace Granston."

"Well, we know who we all are," Grace Granston said with a laugh before hugging her son. Tall and slim, Grace had a warm friendly face framed by short brown hair touched with silver. "Now, let's go inside to get acquainted."

Micah inwardly cringed. The hardest part was coming up, and she glanced at Rob for some sign of encouragement.

"It'll be okay." He mouthed the words to her without saying them while he held her hand warmly in his. They followed the older couple into the house.

"This way, dear," Grace said. "I was hoping Micah would help me with the salad. It will give us a chance to talk before everyone else arrives. Rob, go visit with your dad for a while. We have work to do in the kitchen."

Rob turned to Micah, giving her a questioning look, and she knew he would stay with her if she preferred not to be alone with his mother so soon. But she nodded her head, letting him know it was okay. This could go better than she'd expected, she hoped.

Rob helped Micah out of her lightweight jacket and added it to his own, placing them both over his arm. "I'm going to put these upstairs in the guest room. Do you want to go with me?" he asked quietly, offering her a brief escape.

"I think I'll stay here," she said, suddenly feeling a little braver than she had since she'd agreed to this meeting. And her answer obviously pleased Rob, if the warmth in his eyes was any indication. He lightly kissed the soft hair at her temple before leaving the two alone.

"What can I do to help, Mrs. Granston?" Micah asked as she followed the older woman into the kitchen.

"Please, call me Grace. 'Mrs. Granston' sounds so formal." She motioned toward a counter. "Want to slice some tomatoes and cucumbers for me?"

"Sure," Micah responded. "Do you have a cutting board?"

"It's right here, dear, and the knives are in that drawer to the left," the older woman said with a smile. "Rob tells us you're a wonderful artist."

"Your son is a very kind man, Grace," she said as she washed her hands at the sink.

"Yes, he is. But he is also very honest and, sometimes, blunt. So, if he says you're talented, it isn't just because you're beautiful—which, by the way, he also mentioned." Grace's hand moved to the stem of the pewter frames of her glasses to adjust them. "And I wouldn't even need these bifocals to see that."

"Thank you," Micah replied quietly, feeling

awkward as she focused on the job at hand. Rinsing and cutting vegetables.

"We have more in common than Rob, you know," Grace told her. "I used to teach school when all three of my kids were young."

"I didn't know that."

"Rob probably didn't think to mention it since it was such a long time ago. I only taught for a couple of years before I decided to stay home with the kids. Ed started making more money by then in his real-estate business, and we didn't really need my income. I helped Ed with the business some from then on, but that was back when women weren't so focused on developing their own careers. It seemed like staying home to raise kids was more respectable then. And being at home seemed logical to me since my kids were so close in age, two years between Rob and Angela, and one year between Angela and Eric. Baby-sitters were never easy to find, so I had my hands full with those three."

Micah tried to imagine Rob and Angela as children together. She hadn't met Eric, the younger brother, yet, so he did not appear in her mental image. "Was Rob the one who made things difficult?" Micah asked with a smile. She could picture him doing exactly that.

"Sometimes. But Eric always played that role more than either of the other two. Although Rob had his moments. Like when he was about five and decided to surprise his dad by painting the garage door for him. The idea was good, he'd heard his father talk about needing to take care of that job, but Rob used model paint. Green, purple, orange. He painted circles, squares and triangles all over the door and spilled paint everywhere.''

Micah laughed and said, ''I probably shouldn't laugh. I doubt that it seemed funny when it happened.''

But Grace was laughing, too, as she took some carrots from a plastic container and dropped them into the grater. ''I don't remember being amused by any of it that day, but Rob's mess didn't upset me as much as Ed's helpful commentary on the incident when he returned home. 'If you'd watch the kids closer, you would not have problems like this to contend with.' Trying to explain to him the daily anguish of raising three preschool children was an impossibility. Kind of like trying to explain the daily joys of it, too, I suppose. You just have to be there to appreciate it.''

Micah added the tomatoes and cucumbers she'd sliced to the salad and tried to picture herself dealing with the joys and challenges of motherhood. Children. Of her own? She didn't think she would ever try that challenge. Or she hadn't thought so. Until recently.

''It sounds like Rob showed some interest in art at an early age by decorating your garage,'' Micah remarked, rinsing the cutting board.

''That and cooking. Once, I found him in the middle of the kitchen floor stirring together a dozen cracked eggs—shells and all—in a skillet. He was preparing dinner for us, or so he claimed. Eggs were all over him, all over the kitchen..."

"Sounds like quite a mess."

"Hmm...you'll be surprised by how difficult it all is when you're going through it, and yet, at the same time, you'll know it's some of the best years of your life. No one can tell you how it will be. You have to feel it for yourself."

"Hi, Micah! Hi, Mom! Turn on the oven. I brought the biscuits you asked for," Angela called out as she and her family burst into the kitchen. Grace shooed Heather away from the plate of freshly baked oatmeal cookies and gave each of her grandchildren a big hug. Then Eric and his wife and daughter joined the group for the day.

At that moment two cats came running out of the hallway and into the middle of the kitchen. A black, long-haired feline with eerie blue eyes, and a short-haired calico.

"Herbie! Hattie!" shrieked Heather, who immediately went in pursuit of the pets with determination. "Here, kitty, kitty, kitty."

"Now, Heather, be nice to Grandma's cats," Grace said. "They just woke up from their nap."

"Another nap, Mother?" Angela said. "Really, that's all those animals do. Where's Ashley, anyway? Still snoozing?"

"Open the basement door, Angela. She's downstairs in the family room. I was afraid she'd get stepped on up here, but if you all promise to be careful—''

"We're not going to kill your kitten, Mom. Relax,'' said the young man who had stepped in the door behind Angela. His voice sounded so like Rob's, Micah knew it had to be his brother.

"I guess I should make some introductions,'' Angela began while opening the door to the basement. "Micah, this is Eric and his wife, Hope, with their baby daughter, Cassie.'' Eric resembled Rob, though his eyes were brown. Hope was a pretty, blue-eyed blonde with a warm smile. Their baby Cassie had her mother's fair coloring and soft blonde curls. "And this is my husband, Dan. And, everyone, this is Micah Shepherd, Rob's girlfriend.''

Micah got through the rather uncomfortable moment all right, although the idea of being called a girlfriend when she was nearing her thirties almost amused her. She hadn't really thought of herself as Rob's "anything'' in particular. She only knew that, deep in her heart, she felt certain she belonged with him, and she didn't think there had been a word invented to define those feelings.

Just then, a tiny long-haired calico kitten with blue eyes scampered across the kitchen floor.

"Oh, she's beautiful!'' Micah exclaimed when the little ball of fluff rubbed around her ankles. The kitten couldn't have been more than eight weeks old and its calico fur and bright baby-blue eyes were an obvious mixture of Herbie and Hattie. "She must belong to them," she thought aloud when the fluffy feline met up with the two older cats, all the while continuing to purr loudly.

"She's the runt of their last litter. And I do mean *last* litter. After having to find homes for twenty kittens over the past couple of years, I decided to have Hattie taken out of the kitty-producing business. Our vet saw to that a few days ago," Grace explained as she tossed the various components of the salad together in a beautifully designed glass bowl. "I love cats dearly, but we've got to stop somewhere. Ashley is the only kitten of theirs I've kept, and she is simply too cute to let go."

"I can see that. She's adorable," Micah said and joined Heather on the floor to pet the animals. Micah scratched the kitten under its chin.

Angela steered her boys out of the kitchen, saying, "Dinner will be ready soon. Now, everybody out so we can finish up in here."

It wasn't long before they were all seated around a large rectangular table, ready to eat. But not before the father, Ed Granston, head of this clan, offered a prayer. When he concluded, Micah looked up and gave a sideways glance with a smile to Rob, who was seated next to her. He winked and leaned near to whisper in her ear, "Relax, you're doing fine."

"All right, you two," the younger brother, Eric, stated. "No whispering at the table. Hope and I weren't allowed to do that when we were dating, and you're not entitled to any special privileges.''

"Shut up, Eric, and pass the potatoes," Rob responded casually, bringing a laugh from their parents.

"It's always good to have everyone squabbling under one roof again, isn't it, dear?'' Ed remarked to his wife.

Then the potatoes were passed, along with the roast beef, carrots, gravy, tossed salad and biscuits. Micah couldn't recall the last time she had enjoyed such a meal or a group of people more than the Granstons. After chocolate cake and oatmeal cookies, Angela, Hope and Micah helped Grace in the kitchen, putting away leftovers and filling the dishwasher.

They talked about teaching, which they all had done at one time or another. The topic of church came up, too, from which Micah determined that most of this family had been Christians for some time. No one commented about Rob's view on the subject except Grace, who said rather wistfully that maybe Micah could get her older son back to church someday. If anyone could, she seemed to believe it would be Micah.

The smile Grace gave to Micah as she made her remarks was one of such warmth and acceptance, Micah wished she could somehow fix it in her mind for days when she needed such gentleness. There seemed to be a chemistry between them. Something in Micah's heart somehow connected her to the older woman. It was a feeling she wanted to remember.

After the kitchen work was finished, Micah held baby Cassie, who was barely six months old, for a while, then played on the living-room floor with Heather, David and Nathan. Ashley, little bit of fluff that she was, stayed around Micah all day, while Herbie and Hattie snoozed away the hours, reclining on the back of the sofa. Ashley interrupted the board game so frequently that, finally, Micah held on to her each time the dice were rolled so she wouldn't go chasing them across the properties, knocking the playing pieces over. Rob was never far from Micah throughout the afternoon and early evening, which bolstered her confidence more than he knew.

When it neared time to go, the goodbyes were made much more easily than the nerve-racking hellos at their arrival. Rob went upstairs to retrieve their jackets from the guest bedroom where everyone had left their coats.

Micah waited at the bottom landing of the staircase until he returned. Rob held the brown jacket up as she turned around, slipping her arms in. He caught her cascade of auburn curls in one hand, pulling it free from the garment and lifting it away from her neck. And in the moment of solitude and darkness on the landing, Rob leaned forward and his mouth seared a path down the delicate cord of Micah's throat and onto the back of her neck, causing a sharp intake of breath from her at the deliciously unexpected contact. But the intimate warmth of his lips against her skin ended abruptly when Angela and Heather came around the corner without warning.

"Bad timing, Liz," Rob remarked with a sheepish smile.

"Looks like I've arrived just in time to save a damsel in distress."

"I'm not so sure I'm in distress," Micah quietly responded. Rob's smile widened in approval of her reply as he placed an arm around Micah's waist.

"All the more reason for my timely arrival," Angela commented, shaking her head in mock disapproval. "I should talk to this young woman before her thinking is any more deluded—"

"Angela," Rob said sharply and then stopped.

Micah, surprised to hear Rob call his sister by any name other than Liz, caught her lower lip between her teeth and didn't utter a sound. An angry word between these two people was something Micah had never expected to hear, and she regretted that her quick remark had played a part in this tense exchange.

Angela immediately patted Heather on the back. "Go on upstairs and get our jackets."

"But, Mommy, I've seen them kiss before. It's no big deal," Heather protested as she started up the steps reluctantly.

"Heather, go," came her mom's response before

she turned to Rob with regret darkening her eyes. "I didn't mean anything—"

Rob's voice was quieter and more controlled when he interrupted her. "Not being a Christian doesn't mean that I have no respect for other—"

"I'm not saying it means anything. It was just a bad joke. Okay? Forget I said it," Angela answered and turned to join her daughter upstairs.

Without further explanation, Rob's hand moved against Micah's back, guiding her toward the front door. "Mom, Dad, we're heading out now."

Grace came out of the kitchen carrying two plates covered with aluminum foil. "Don't forget these leftovers. You can heat them for dinner tomorrow night." Grace handed the items to Rob as he kissed her on the cheek.

"Thanks, Mom. Tell Dad goodnight for us. I think he fell asleep in the recliner."

"Well, that's nothing new, is it?" she commented before turning her attention to Micah. "It's been wonderful having you with us, dear. Please come back soon."

Micah smiled and thanked Grace for the day she'd allowed Micah to share with the family. Then Ashley, the kitten, came scrambling to Micah's feet, purring and rubbing around her ankles. "I like you, too, little cat," Micah said when she knelt to touch the soft fur. When Micah stood up again, Rob disappeared briefly into the living room to say goodbye to the rest of the family. It was then that Grace gave

Micah a generous hug, which was readily returned by an appreciative Micah.

"You know, dear," Grace began in a voice that was little more than a whisper, "Rob thinks he's discovered you all on his own. But I believe you are a gift from the Lord. And someday he'll see that."

Micah, stunned by the comment, could only smile and thank Rob's mother again for her kindness before Rob reappeared, and with his hand on her elbow, ushered her out of his parents' home and into the car.

"Whew," he said as they headed down the street toward home. "Quite a day, huh?"

"I loved it, as soon as the getting acquainted part was over. And your mom, she's wonderful."

Rob reached across the seat, taking Micah's left hand into his grasp. "I knew she'd be good for you."

"She's quite a departure from what I'm used to. With my mother, there's always some wall, something between us that's not right. It's hard to explain. I think I'm simply not the kind of daughter she wanted."

"Well, then, she wanted the wrong kind of daughter."

"Maybe," Micah replied and decided to change the subject. "Angela's husband didn't say much all day."

"Dan has always been quiet, but with his drinking problem... He's made life hard at times for Liz and the kids. He doesn't feel very comfortable at family dinners right now.''

''How do your parents feel about him?''

''Unconditional love,'' Rob responded with a negative tone. ''They want him to stay sober and keep his family happy, but they'll love him no matter what. He's the prodigal son they watch and wait for.''

''I thought that was your role to play,'' Micah offered softly. She had thought that about him that very day.

''Now, it's Dan's,'' Rob answered quietly, and they rode in silence for the next several minutes.

''Rob,'' Micah began, ''you can tell me to mind my own business if you want to and I won't be offended, but what happened back there between you and Angela? I've never known you to be angry with her about anything.''

Rob didn't respond right away, and Micah expected him to choose not to tell her.

''What you saw back there between us was guilt. Plain and simple.''

Micah frowned in misunderstanding, but refrained from asking further questions. If he wanted to tell her, he would without prompting.

''Micah...Liz was pregnant when she married Dan.''

''I didn't know,'' was the only appropriate comment she could think to make.

''Well, that makes you one of the few people who

didn't. For my family, Liz's condition was quite scandalous at the time."

"But that was years ago. What difference could it make now?" And, Micah considered silently, if the Granstons reacted badly to that situation, what would they think of her own past?

"None, really," Rob replied. "I don't care much for Dan. It's difficult to feel brotherly toward someone who has caused Liz so much heartache."

It was not Rob's statement as much as the strain in his voice that puzzled Micah. What was it that she detected? Anger, regret, guilt?

"I get the feeling that somehow, in all of this, you blame yourself," she commented.

"Liz would never have gotten involved with him if I'd been paying enough attention to stop it. She's always looked up to me more than she should. But all this started right after Nick died...and that's when my own life came unglued for a couple of years. And Liz, she paid the price for some of it."

"Maybe you should be a little more forgiving of yourself. You know? I mean, maybe your sister really fell in love with Dan and would have made the same decisions whether or not you approved of him."

"I don't know. I don't think so, but she loves him now. And so do Mom and Dad. They'd all be happier with me if I did, too."

"So, you're trying?"

"If I could just like him, that would be a start,"

he said with a smile. They pulled onto Micah's street and into their usual parking spot. "That's enough about my family. Tell me about your mother's letter."

"It was nothing, really. Just a stay-in-touch letter she sends every now and then. You know, the 'I'm fine, how are you?' kind."

"That's all?" Rob asked, skepticism obvious in his tone.

"That and will I be moving soon? Or have I found a place I can make permanent? Have I spoken to Dad—"

"Have you?"

"No," she responded.

"Could you? If you wanted to?"

"Yes, but he wouldn't be interested," she stated and offered nothing more.

Rob hesitated, apparently hoping she would continue, but she only suggested they go inside her apartment, which they did, in silence.

Once inside, Micah began to slip out of her spring jacket, when Rob reached toward her, sliding it easily down her arms. She turned to face him, wanting very much to be in his arms, but she noticed he still wore his jacket. She looked up at him with questioning eyes.

"I'm not staying long," he explained and remained in the entryway as Micah shut the closet door and leaned back against it with a sigh of disappointment.

"But we haven't been alone for more than a few minutes all day," she said.

"It's better for you that we haven't been," he stated gently.

"But I liked what you were doing to my neck when Angela interrupted us." She smiled and moved close to him, placing both hands on his chest.

"I doubt that you liked it as much as I did," he remarked before taking her fully into his arms. "Which is exactly why I should be leaving now."

"Rob, don't go," she pleaded and gave him a soft kiss on the cheek. "Not yet."

Rob's eyes darkened as he studied Micah's steady gaze. Then he kissed her once, too lightly, on the lips, and Micah surprised herself with her eager reaction to the brief touch of his lips against hers. She raised up, inviting a more intimate contact, which evoked a quiet groan from him. Then his mouth recaptured hers with a possessiveness he'd not allowed between them before tonight. And Micah responded, meeting his demanding kiss with all the yearning she'd felt for him since the very beginning now playing out in this one exchange. When Rob's mouth abandoned the softness of her lips to trail kisses down her chin, jawline and the slender column of her throat, she tilted her head to the side, exposing more soft skin for his exploration. And the thought of not having this man—*never* having this man—pierced her heart, and she moaned softly in a bittersweet mixture of the sadness of letting him go and the pleasure he offered her. Now. Always.

"Micah," he breathed her name as he pulled slightly away from her. "I'm trying to be a gentleman, but I'm having trouble remembering how to do that."

"And I'm not exactly helping, am I?" she commented. Taking a deep breath, she stepped away from him.

"No, you're not," he agreed, letting her slip from his arms. "And Liz isn't around to discourage us."

Micah smiled. "Maybe we should call her. She might come over to supervise."

"I'm sure she would, and she'd probably bring all three kids. That would cool things down considerably."

"But please stay for a while," she said. "I could make some coffee. We could sit at the table and talk."

"No, it's time for me to leave." He kissed her forehead lightly. "Because talking isn't what I had in mind," he admitted with a disturbing smile.

Micah trailed a finger across Rob's lips. "I guess I've known all along that I'd never really have you. Not the way I want to," she stated softly. "But it's never hurt as much as it does now."

"There will be a right time for us, but this isn't it," he assured her.

"There'll never be a right time," she said more to herself than to him. "Because being husband and wife is the only right time for this, and we will never be that.''

''Why?'' he asked suddenly. ''I've never been as sure of anything in my life as I am of us. We belong together, and whether you'll admit it or not, I know you feel it, too.''

''It just can't happen. This was wrong from the beginning. I was foolish to let it go so far.''

''Micah, I don't care what the obstacles are. We can work through them.''

''No, we can't—'' she insisted.

''Yes, we can, and we will. I don't care if you *are* married. I'll get you out of it. Divorces, dissolutions…it's not as difficult as it seems.''

''Married?'' She laughed at the thought, but then she saw the sincerity in his direct gaze. ''What would make you think I'm married?''

''It doesn't matter.''

''It matters to me! Why would you say such a thing? Do you think I could have a husband stashed away somewhere, yet get involved with you? Love you the way I do?''

''Things happen. Even to Christians. People sometimes do things they never dreamed they would do.''

''I wouldn't be unfaithful to a husband! I don't care how much I wanted someone else.''

''We haven't exactly committed adultery yet,'' Rob stated.

''But there's more to unfaithfulness than falling

into bed with someone. You and I have spent *hours* together. We've laughed and eaten and held hands...and kissed until I felt I could almost die from wanting you. Do you think I would do that if I'd promised my life to some other man?''

''Micah—''

''And if you think that, how could you trust me to belong to you? All you'd have is a relationship with a woman who has already cheated on one husband.''

He studied her thoughtfully for a moment. ''I know you, Micah. Regardless of what's happened in the past, what we have together is real. I'd take my chances.'' Rob turned and walked to the nearby bookcase, and pulled a small white Bible from the highest shelf. ''I suppose most kids get one of these as a graduation gift from their church, a Bible with their name engraved in gold letters on the cover. But why does yours read, 'Micah Marie Jamison'?''

''You had no right to go through my things—''

''I'm sorry if it seems as if I pried, but I need to know,'' he interrupted. ''Why is your name Shepherd now? What happened in the last decade to account for the difference?''

''Well, certainly not a marriage,'' she replied and sank into the chair behind her. There was no avoiding this subject now. ''I had it changed, legally changed, when I became an adult.''

He returned the leather-bound book to the shelf. ''How did your parents react to the news?''

"My father asked me to do it. Ordered me, actually." Micah answered the questions, knowing there would be many more.

"Why, Micah? Why would a parent do that to a child?"

"Because our name had gained a lot of notoriety in the community. In the whole area, really," she said and sadly shook her head. "The trial you've asked me about was my father's, as I've told you."

Rob stood silently watching her begin to explain her past.

"Like I told you, my father didn't just steal some money, he embezzled it—lots of it—from the company he worked for. He's still in prison as far as I know. Mother and Father suffered through a terrible trial."

"And so did you," he added.

"Yes, well, the publicity was heavy. Everyone knew about it. And it was far more scandalous than what happened with Angela and Dan, believe me. I wouldn't want to see your family's reaction to this—"

"I'll take care of that. Tell me the rest."

Micah folded her hands in her lap to steady them and looked down at the floor rather than into Rob's eyes. "We had a beautiful home then...new cars, clothes, vacations several times a year...it was a lavish lifestyle. And, apparently, at least some of it was financed with money that wasn't ours. Anyway, once my father's trial was under way, there were stories and photos of us in the local news, coming and going to the courthouse." She paused and rubbed her arms to wish away a sudden chill. "I lost everything. My parents, my home, my friends. I was only seventeen, Rob. It frightened me."

"Is that when your mother left?"

"She stayed until the trial ended. Then she left for Paris with a friend. A man...who I think was her 'friend' long before they arrived in France. She asked me to go along, but I refused. We'd never gotten along well together, and without Dad as a buffer between us, I knew it wouldn't work."

"What did you do? I mean, you were just a kid."

"I went to a church I had visited a few times earlier that year. And I just sat there in a pew one afternoon, wondering what I was going to do. A woman came up to me and wanted to talk. She turned out to be the pastor's wife. I think the more we talked, the more I cried. And pretty soon, she was crying, too. Oh, Rob, she was so kind, caring, compassionate.... She was everything I needed her to be."

Rob moved to Micah's side and placed a hand on her shoulder without saying a word. His touch against her arm was gentle, and she reached up to take his hand.

"She was so helpful and patient, listening to me ramble on and on. I used to think I'd be a pastor's wife someday...and be just like she was so I could help people who needed it. I know this sounds crazy, but she offered to let me stay with them.''

''There's nothing crazy about it, Micah. God helped you through her.''

''But she didn't know anything more about me than what I told her and what the papers said. Yet, she took me into that parsonage with her three kids and her husband, and they accepted me as though I belonged there. I stayed with them for the next two months while I finished school. Then I found a job as a secretary and a cheap efficiency apartment in the area so I could be on my own. But that family made the difference in what my life turned out to be,'' Micah continued with a smile. ''They are the reason I accepted the Lord into my life. They offered me compassion when I thought I'd never find it anywhere, and I wanted to be like them. I still do.''

''That's one of the reasons I love you so,'' Rob said, his voice edged with sadness.

''But I've told you from the beginning we shouldn't start this. You thought if I loved you, it would change things,'' Micah gently explained. ''But I do, and it doesn't change anything.''

Rob touched her face and the tenderness in his expression was almost unbearable for Micah to see. ''It won't rewrite history, if that's what you mean,'' he said. ''It can't turn your dad into an honest man or make your mother into the maternal type. But it doesn't have to be the end of us. We can live with this.''

"No, we can't. I won't," she stated emphatically.

"But, have you told me everything? Is that all there is to it?"

"Isn't that enough?" Micah responded, deliberately not answering the question.

"You've had a horrible experience, and I know your father is in prison...but if I can accept that without reservation, why won't you let me? This career doesn't mean—"

"It's not just your profession. It just can't work for us. It might be fine in the beginning, but there will come a day when you realize what a mistake you've made—"

"Then what do you want from me, Micah? Here? Now? And nothing more?"

"That's all we can have."

"You can't give me today and expect me not to want tomorrow. That's too much to ask."

"That's all I have to give you," she whispered, trying not to cry as she pulled her hand away from his grasp.

"Did you think I could be with you and not fall in love? Micah, I've loved you almost from the beginning."

"You want what you think I am...not the real me. You need someone who can be a part of your family. Someone who will give you children. I won't."

Micah hated what she'd done to him when he looked at her in disbelief. She knew the hurt she had dealt him; it was her pain, too.

"Why wouldn't you have a child with me?" he asked quietly.

"I don't know how to be a good parent. My mother *never* loved me. Not from my earliest memory. She only stays in touch with me out of a sense of duty. I won't pass that legacy on to a next generation."

"Micah, you're a *teacher!* I've seen you with Heather and the boys, and you have all the right instincts with kids. There's nothing maternal lacking in you."

"But you don't know how it feels. You have your family, the things you've learned from them, their presence in your life, their love."

"They'll love you, too. They'll be your family."

"Why should they?"

"Because I love you. My mom is already crazy about you," he protested.

"She won't be when she knows what a liability I can be to her son. I've already had one mom protect her son from me. I don't intend to go through that again."

"When did that happen? You've never mentioned—"

"It's not important. What matters is that you find someone who will give you the respectable life that you deserve…with lots of kids so you can have Sunday get-togethers like your parents do and Thanksgiving dinners and eat fruitcake in December—" Her wavering words broke off with a cry, and she stood up and walked to the front door. Turning the knob and breaking the heart that beat within her, she pulled open the door.

Rob stood by the chair for a minute, watching her in a mixture of disbelief and mounting frustration. "Micah, don't do this. I don't care about family dinners—"

"Yes, you do. They're part of you as much as my upbringing is a part of me. This was wrong, Rob, from the beginning. I'm sorry."

"It was never wrong. Not with us," he insisted. His eyes misted with tears, and Micah looked away as he continued, "But I can't fight you every step of the way. This hurts too much."

"Then don't." She choked the words out.

"All right, you win," he conceded bitterly. "There's obviously more to this story than you're telling me, because this isn't enough to keep us apart. Are you going to give me the missing piece of this puzzle before I walk out of here?"

Micah shook her head no without looking up into the frustration she knew she'd find in his eyes.

"Then I'll leave you alone with your miserable past or whatever it is you want to hold on to more than you want me. I didn't accept inadequate answers from God, and I won't accept them from you." Then he walked away.

Micah leaned back against the wall and slid down, inches at a time, until she sank onto the floor and, burying her face in her hands, wept inconsolably.

* * *

The days passed slowly and the nights even more slowly. Micah purposely avoided her apartment as much as she could, assuming Rob would return. But if he had, there was no indication of it. No notes, no calls, no messages on the answering machine. Nothing.

Teaching the next several days kept her busy most of the time, and Angela didn't mention the breakup. Micah spent some time painting in the park when weather permitted. The summer-festival season for her artwork would begin over the long holiday weekend, and she needed to prepare for her display. The country-church scene she'd started months ago, before her weeks with Rob, had been sadly neglected. But she started working on it again, and it began to take shape the way she had envisioned it, exactly as it had looked that first afternoon she saw it—a welcoming place that was in need of a good paint job. Suddenly, Micah missed that little church in the woods. She felt almost homesick for it. Maybe she'd go back there this Sunday. It had been so long since she'd visited. But she had always supposed Rob would go with her one day. It was the kind of place he would like.

Thursday evening came and she dawdled around the neighborhood Laundromat nearly twice as long as necessary rather than hurry home to a lonely apartment. Carole came in with her own dirty laundry just as Micah began folding the dish towels.

"Hiya!" Carole said as she plopped her basketful

of clothes onto the floor. "Why haven't you called? I wanted to know how your day with Rob's family went."

"Sorry. I haven't felt very chatty these days." Micah knew Carole would talk about the cute accountant she had been seeing, and she did not want to hear it so soon after losing Rob. "So, how are you?" she asked and braced herself.

"I'm okay, and I'm learning a lot about finances as well as other things," Carole answered with a mischievous expression as she dumped an odd assortment of clothing into the washer. "How did family day with the Granstons go?"

"Wonderful," Micah replied with a sad sigh.

"I see. And that explains why you look so miserable?" Carole remarked with a frown. "I don't understand you. How could you have a guy like that and be so unhappy?"

"We're not seeing each other any longer," Micah said and continued folding her towels.

"Not seeing each other!" Carole exclaimed so loudly other people in the Laundromat looked over at them. "After all you've been through with him, now it's over? Are you serious?"

Micah reached for a washcloth. "Yes, I'm serious."

Carole placed her hands on the table and pushed herself up to sit on top of the folding table, sitting directly beneath a posted sign: Do Not Sit On Machines Or Table. "I should have known something was wrong. I haven't heard from you for days."

"It just won't work, Carole. No matter how hard we try."

"You've got to be kidding. You saw each other almost nonstop for weeks, and now it's just over. There's something you're not telling me."

"No juicy details to tell you. It simply wasn't meant to be." Micah stacked the last of her dish towels onto the top of a nearly full basket. "Sorry to disappoint you."

"But—" Carole stopped abruptly as Micah's green gaze flashed a warning that temporarily halted her friend's relentless prying.

"I'm glad things are working out for you and your accountant."

"He has a really nice friend. We could introduce you to him," Carole said.

Suddenly, all Micah wanted to do was go home. "I don't think so, Carole. Thanks, anyway."

"You're really in love with Rob," Carole stated.

Micah shrugged. "It doesn't matter now. I'll see you later."

"I'll never understand you, Micah Shepherd. I've watched you date guys over the past two years that you didn't care much for, and then you find one who is right for you and you tell me, 'it just won't work.'" Carole was quiet for a moment. "You're the one who ended it."

"Yes," Micah answered. "Someone had to."

"And we're back to him being a lawyer again, aren't we? Are you in trouble with the law or something?" Carole asked quietly. "I mean, I wouldn't tell anybody and that would explain—"

"No," Micah replied briskly. "Don't be ridiculous. I'm not on a Most Wanted poster anywhere." Picking up her overflowing laundry basket, she started toward the door.

"Micah, you're making a serious mistake, and by the time you realize it, it may be too late. Trust me on this," Carole responded, watching Micah leave.

"Thanks, Carole. I know you mean well, but that's just the way it is. I'll call you in a day or two." Micah backed through the double doors. "When I do, let's talk about something other than Rob Granston, attorney-at-law. Okay?"

Chapter Ten

The boxes of chocolate displayed in the window of the tiny candy shop caught Micah's attention, and she stopped to view the selection. Hiking her book bag over one shoulder, she slid her thumbs into the belt loops of her jeans. Mrs. Poe loved chocolates and tomorrow was her birthday. And this was the first edible thing Micah had seen for nearly two weeks that actually looked good to her.

"Micah!" Carole stepped out of the shop. "I thought that was you."

"Hello," Micah responded, glad to see her friend. She could buy a gift later. She'd rather talk to Carole now.

"Want some?" Carole held out a small bag of chocolates. "They have peanuts in them."

"Sure," Micah said and reached into the sack for a sample. "What about your diet?"

"It was successful!" Carole laughed. "I lost seven pounds. See?" She turned around to display a shapely figure. "A little chocolate never hurt anyone."

Micah smiled.

"Where have you been hiding yourself lately? I haven't seen you since that night at the Laundromat." Carole pushed a few stray blond strands of hair from her forehead. "You are a hard person to get in touch with, and I'm getting tired of talking to your machine."

"I've been teaching and painting, getting ready for the festivals this summer."

"Are you going to do that again this year? Traipse around to all those hot, crowded carnivals drawing pictures?" Carole wrinkled her nose in obvious distaste.

"They're called caricatures, and, yes, I am. I enjoy it."

"Why you like sitting in all that humidity in those crowded places, I'll never understand."

"The caricatures are fun to do, I meet some interesting people and I make pretty good money," Micah explained to her frowning friend.

"You could take a full-time teaching position if you want to, Micah. You've had plenty of opportunity. You only need to be willing to commit yourself. Rob was saying just last night—"

"Rob?" Micah cut off Carole's words.

Carole popped a piece of candy into her mouth.

"I've seen him a few times. I didn't think you'd mind."

Micah stood nearly speechless for a moment, staring at her friend's unconcerned expression. "No...I..." She paused. Why should she mind? She had ended her relationship with him. She had no hold on his future. "Why should I mind?" she asked quietly.

"My thought exactly. You said you had no plans to see him again, so when he called the first time—"

"The first time?" Micah repeated. "You've been seeing him regularly?"

"Kind of. He called me not long after the talk you and I had at the Laundromat."

"What happened to the cute accountant?" Micah inquired as she recalled a portion of their conversation from that evening.

The shopkeeper of the candy store in front of which they still stood turned out the lights in the display window. It was nearly five o'clock.

"Let's go to my car," Carole said, pointing across the street to a small automobile. "It looks like they're closing up shop here." They began crossing the street as Carole answered, "The accountant was fun for a while. That's all."

"And Rob?" When they reached the car, Micah leaned against it, waiting for Carole's response. "You always said he was more my type than yours."

"He still is, actually, but I'm beginning to think

your type of men are better bets than mine. I've wound up with too many losers.'' Carole folded down the top of the candy sack. ''Rob is an interesting man.''

''You should know. You dated him before I even met him.'' Micah's reply rang a little sharper than intended.

''I went out to lunch with him back then. One time, Micah. That's all.'' Carole leaned through the opened car window and placed what remained of her purchase on the front seat. ''I thought then he'd make a good match for you, but since you're not interested... Anyway, he called me, and I reconsidered.''

''So now you're doing more than eating lunch with him,'' Micah commented, shielding her eyes from the glare of the setting sun.

''Yes, I've had dinner with him, too,'' Carole replied.

''And breakfast?''

Carole's eyes flickered with amusement at Micah's inquisition. ''Not yet. You really are jealous, aren't you?''

''Why should I be jealous? I'm the one who ended it, remember?''

''I remember, Rob remembers,'' Carole said. ''But do you? If you're the one who sent him away, why are you now upset that someone else wants him?''

Micah's cool green gaze eyed Carole cautiously

while asking herself the same question. Why did she care?

"He only talks about you, Micah. He's just using me to get to you, and I'm going along with it. See what a good friend you have in me? I'm so determined to get you two together that I'm sticking myself right in the middle of this mess. Why don't you call him? You could still patch things up."

Micah frowned at Carole's suggestion. "I don't think so, Carole. You are the one he's seeing."

"And *you* are the one he *wants* to see," Carole added, smiling at Micah's frowning face. "He's a nice guy, Micah, and I like him, but there's nothing going on between us. I just wanted to make you see what you're giving up. Call him. Please, Micah. Take a chance on this man."

Micah shook her head and lowered her gaze to the brick pavement beneath her feet. Here she stood, questioning her best friend about things that were none of her business…jealous over a man she had sent away. If only *she* could get away.…

"I think I'll go up to that cabin for a few days. Remember, that one we rented last Christmas?" Micah said. Maybe a change of scenery, even a temporary one, would help.

"Call Rob. See if he can go with you," Carole offered and, with a smile, added, "you have my permission."

Micah smiled back. "I'm sorry I was so sharp

with you. I had no right to pry into your private life.''

''Hey, what are friends for?'' Carole replied in a lighthearted voice while climbing into her automobile. ''Want a ride?''

''No, thanks. I need the exercise.'' Micah began to walk away from the car.

''Are you really going up to that isolated cabin? All by yourself?'' Carole asked with a frown. ''Do you think that's a good idea?''

''I'll be fine. I need to go alone to do some thinking. Next time, I'll invite you to go along.''

''I wasn't thinking of myself, Micah. Rob is the person you should take.''

Micah shook her head again. She couldn't go back now. Her decision had already been made. ''See you later, Carole.''

''Forget he's a lawyer for the weekend. Pretend he's an art instructor, or a picture framer, or unemployed! You'd like that, wouldn't you?''

Micah wished it could be that simple. Why couldn't he be something other than what he was? And why couldn't she? Why couldn't the fact that he was no longer a Christian be enough reason for her to let him go? ''I'll phone you next week,'' she called to her friend and began walking away.

''I'm telling you, you'd better grab him while he's still available. If I spend much more time with him, I might issue a breakfast invitation.'' Carole's words were a warning but spoken with a genuine smile. Still, Micah wasn't sure if Carole had only been teasing as she watched her friend's car disappear around the corner.

Deciding on flowers for her landlady's gift, Micah stopped at a nearby florist and purchased a small bouquet that she delivered to Mrs. Poe before heading back to her own apartment. She found her suitcase underneath the bed, and she started packing. A pair of shorts, her new jeans, a couple of shirts and some clean undergarments. She didn't need much. The thick mystery book lying on the floor by the side of her bed made it into the luggage, but only temporarily. Micah quickly removed it from the bag. Being alone in that cabin could be eerie enough at night. She didn't need any added effects. She glanced through the stack of reading material beside her bed, looking for something else to take. She found another mystery and a romance.

"Great," she said aloud to herself. "Just what I need. A love story." Pushing that book aside, she gathered up a couple of recent magazines and tossed them in on top of her clothes. Then she saw the book of devotions she'd been reading the other night and added it to the top of her pile. "This should help. I'll read some every morning and night," she reasoned. In little more than half an hour, she had everything she needed packed and loaded into the car. A quick call to the rental office confirmed the availability of the cabin she wanted. She would pick up a few groceries and take off first thing in the morning.

May. A lovely time of year and Micah's favorite month. Yellow and red tulips bloomed around the spacious front porch of the cabin nestled in the woods. Micah eased her rambling old station wagon through the secluded trees and parked close to the back door so she could unload her belongings easily.

After going inside and wiping away some of the dust and cobwebs, Micah carried her easel and half finished canvas into a work area she selected in the living room. Returning to the kitchen she found the few modern conveniences there covered with a layer of dust. She had not been at this haven in the woods since Christmas, when she and Carole had enjoyed the holidays here together. A forlorn piece of tinsel lay on the large braided rug, a glimmering reminder of that long-ago holiday. Micah leaned over, picked up the scrap and tossed it into the trash and wondered if anyone had rented this place since that December vacation.

Crash! Micah jumped when a picture frame that she had leaned against the wall fell over, hitting the hardwood floor. After inspecting it and finding it damaged, she moved it to a better spot. Then she decided to check out the rest of the rooms. The two tiny bedrooms upstairs offered more than enough room for Micah and her belongings. The kitchen, living room and bathroom downstairs were all in good repair, and Micah switched on the refrigerator. She left her groceries in the ice chest until the temperature in the refrigerator was cool enough to maintain the food.

Pulling back the colorful striped kitchen curtains, she stared out into bright sunshine. The weekend promised to be a beautiful one, and this first day of it passed slowly and leisurely, much to Micah's delight. A week of rowdy elementary-school students with little interest in schoolwork had frayed Micah's nerves. And there had been those two night classes to teach, one to attend and a pottery course she helped with…and no Rob. That was the part she wasn't sure she would ever grow accustomed to.

Dusk settled over the area, and Micah placed the kettle on the stove to make a pot of tea. Then she began making a peanut butter and jelly sandwich. A knock outside the front door startled her, almost frightened her. Who could be up here in this remote part of the woods? Maybe it was Carole. She knew Micah planned to come here. Maybe she decided to drop in for a visit. Micah peeked through the window and saw a raccoon scampering off the front porch and a flowerpot lying on the wooden floor, toppled by the clumsy visitor.

''Frightened by a little critter like you,'' Micah said, laughing as she cleaned up the spilled plant and went back indoors to finish her sandwich.

She had just turned off the burner under the tea kettle when she heard a car pull into the gravel driveway. She pulled back a curtain and looked out. And saw Rob.

"Carole," she said aloud to the friend who was nowhere to be seen. "What have you done now?" She closed the curtain and headed toward the front door, pulling it open just as Rob stepped onto the porch.

"This is a surprise," she stated softly and looked into his direct gaze as he approached the screen door. But she quickly lowered her eyes to the collar of his shirt to avoid confronting the sadness she'd seen, sadness she'd left there, sadness she shared.

"How are you?" he asked quietly, easily.

"Okay..." Micah responded, "I guess. How about you?"

"I've been better," Rob replied, rubbing a hand against the back of his neck in a weary movement. "It's a long drive from Columbus."

"Uh-huh, it is," she commented and bit her lower lip, restraining words she dare not say. Not now.

"I don't suppose you bothered to listen to a weather report before you came running up here for the weekend?"

"No," Micah answered, feeling suddenly childish for not having thought of it. One look toward the darkening skies told her she should have done so. "Is that why you're here?" she questioned him quietly. "To give me details on the weather?"

Rob's laugh sounded harsh. Bitter. "Yep," he said. "I spent an hour and a half driving up here to give you a five-day forecast.'' Pain flashed through the blue eyes Micah, once again, looked into, and she knew he was as disappointed by the things she didn't say as he was with those she said. He turned to go.

"Rob, don't—'' She pushed open the heavy screen door that had stood between them and stepped out onto the porch. The door slammed shut behind her.

He stopped and turned back to face her. "Carole called me at the office. If your cabin had a phone, she could have told you herself. There are severe storm warnings for tonight, and she's worried about you being alone in this isolated place all weekend.''

"What Carole wants is for you to spend the weekend here with me, as though that would solve all of our problems.''

Rob shook his head and looked out toward his car. "That would cause more problems for us than it would solve. I came here to see if I could talk you into going home. To your home, by yourself…the way you like it to be.''

"It's not the way I like it—it's the way it has to be,'' Micah replied.

"So you say,'' he commented. "Do you need help carrying things to your car? I assume you brought some paintings to work on—''

"I'm not going home, Rob. I'm not afraid of thunder and lightning.'' What she feared more was the tranquillity she could find in this man's arms.

Anger flickered through his gaze again just as Micah knew it would, and she was relieved at its return. Anger proved much easier to send away than tenderness.

"Okay, Micah," he remarked. "Have it your way. Have your whole life your own way. I don't care anymore."

Rob's words, cold and deliberate, stung her and tears flooded her eyes as he turned to go.

Micah watched him get into his car and drive away. What had she expected would happen? Nothing had changed. Nothing would change that could make a difference until one of them stopped loving. And, maybe, Rob already had. She held her arms to her stomach, rubbing them to fight off the chill of another parting.

She sat down on the top step leading from the porch and prayed for Rob. "He's angry, he will probably drive too fast and the sky looks so stormy. Please let him make it home safely, Lord. He shouldn't have come up here. If Carole would only mind her own business and keep her nose out of mine...." Dusk was settling in with darkness not far behind, and the storm clouds created an eerie, lonely atmosphere...as if anything could make her feel lonelier than she always felt when she was no longer with Rob. After losing track of time, she finally stood up and went back inside the cabin. Her painting of the country church seemed to demand her attention. The sign she'd added to the lawn needed the name 'Pinewood' painted on it, but she had decided not to do so until everything else was completed. That could be the finishing touch to the piece of art that had easily become her favorite.

So, pushing other thoughts aside, she concentrated for a short time on the steeple and the various shades of gray she was experimenting with. Gray. An appropriate choice, she thought, considering her mood.

She stretched out on the couch later and switched off the lamp. Nestling down into the warmth of the soft afghan, she slept peacefully until a sharp noise awakened her. Thunder. Loud and rumbling. And flashes of lightning.

"Rain," Micah mumbled, thinking of her car windows. She wondered if she'd shut them. And if she'd left any of her paintings on the seat. Micah bolted from the couch and ran to the front door and out into the torrential downpour that hit at the same moment her hand yanked open the driver's door of the station wagon. She closed the only window she'd left open and turned to run back through the rain to the cabin when another crack of lightning startled her. She lost her footing on the wood steps leading to the porch and went down, hitting her head against the stairs. Pain shot through her, and then...nothing. Nothing but darkness.

Chapter Eleven

Micah opened her eyes. Shades of green surrounded her. Bedspread, carpeting, drapes. Pulling the covers up close to her neck, she tried to remember, but a pounding headache dulled her thinking. The hospital…she'd been there but it hadn't looked like this. Micah recalled the warm water of a shower. She blinked and remained still, trying to piece together her memories of last night. Then, rolling over onto her side, she saw him. Rob sat, sleeping, in a chair in the corner of the room. He stirred from his uncomfortable position. His clothes rumpled and hair disheveled, she watched him slowly awaken.

"'Morning," he offered quietly as his eyes met hers, and, slowly, he stood up.

"Hi," she responded in a soft voice. "Where are

we?'' The pain in the side of her face startled her. She raised a hand to her temple.

''My apartment. I didn't want you at your place alone.''

''But you shouldn't have slept in that uncomfortable chair—''

''My bed was already taken.'' One corner of his mouth turned up in a wry smile. ''And you weren't so willing to let me leave the room last night,'' he explained in a gentle tone.

''I'm sorry.''

''Don't be. There was no way I would have let you out of my sight anyway.''

Micah tried to smile, but the pain was too sharp.

''It probably feels worse than it looks,'' he said and sat down on the edge of the bed. ''Remember what happened?''

''I slipped and fell. I think the step was slick.''

''It was pouring, Micah. What were you doing outside in the rain?''

''I went out to close my car windows…I think. I must have hit my head against the porch floor when I fell, but I don't know what happened right after that. The next thing I can recall is being at the hospital.'' She touched Rob's arm. ''And you were there…but…how? Why?''

''I found you lying outside in the rain.''

''But you'd left. You said you didn't care anymore.''

Rob covered her hand with his own. ''I had driven

about halfway home when I made a U-turn and headed back to the cabin. I do care, Micah. Telling you that I didn't was a lie. And I didn't want that to be the last thing said between us. Not after all we've had together.''

"Oh, Rob, I love you so," she offered slowly and buried her face in his shoulder as he gathered her into his arms.

"I know you do," he said quietly, his mouth moving warmly against her hair as he held her close. "I love you, too. More than I can say."

Micah nodded her head, rubbing her aching temple against his cotton shirt. She moaned softly in response to the pain in her head.

"Your stitches," he remarked, pulling slightly away from her. "Don't lean into me like that or your forehead will hurt even more than it already does."

"How many stitches?" She hadn't even thought to look at her face yet. But, just then, she glanced up at the reflection in the large mirror above a dresser and saw the bluish-purplish mark across her forehead, temple and down the corner of one eye. "Oh…Rob. I look awful."

"You look awfully good to me. Cuts heal—bruises fade." He leaned near to tease her ear with a light kiss. "You have four stitches there at the top of your forehead. They took X rays at the hospital, and everything looked all right so you'll be fine in a few days. And you're staying here until I'm sure you're okay."

"I can go home and take care of myself."

"Nope," he answered flatly. "I'll be here all day, and when I go into the office in the morning, Mom is coming over."

"That's not necessary—"

"I'm the one who spoke with your doctor last night," he interrupted in a gentle, but firm tone. "He agreed it's necessary, and also said you should just follow orders for a change."

"That doesn't come naturally to me, you know," she responded and watched his smile widen.

"Tell me about it," he remarked with a laugh and squeezed her shoulder gently. "Your doctor said you should be checked on frequently for the next couple of days. So I am going to see to it that you are cared for properly—so don't argue about it. Want something to drink? Coffee? Juice?"

"Orange juice would be great."

"Okay. I'll be back in a minute."

Rob disappeared through the doorway as Micah inspected her injuries more closely in the nearby mirror. She raised a hand to touch the bruised area and winced at a new stab of pain.

"Feels pretty bad?" Rob asked when he returned with her drink.

She took the glass he offered. "Just the worst headache I've ever had in my life."

"Take it easy today. I'll make some scrambled eggs if you want them."

"No, thanks, I'm not hungry. Just tired."

"Then rest. And don't worry about your paintings. Liz and Dan went up to the cabin after I called them from the hospital last night. They packed up your belongings, turned in the key and brought your car home." Rob smiled. "Sometimes Dan's not such a bad brother-in-law after all."

"But what an inconvenience for them, Rob. Driving all the way up there—"

"Liz owes me. I'm the best spur-of-the-moment baby-sitter she's ever found." He looked toward her suitcase which was across the room. "They brought your things here, and Liz helped you shower and change clothes."

Micah raised a hand to her throat. "My locket—"

"It's here," Rob responded as he pulled the piece of jewelry from his pocket. He reached forward to put the delicate chain around her neck and fasten the clasp. "It came off in the emergency room, and one of the nurses gave it to me. She thought I was your husband," he added. A silent sadness darkened his gaze when Micah glanced up at him, and he didn't give her a chance to respond. "Can you remember much about the hospital? We were there for hours."

"I remember most of it now," she said. "Thank you for taking care of everything...." she touched his hand "...for taking care of me." Micah smiled when the warmth she had missed returned to his eyes.

He nodded. "You're welcome. You're also very stubborn, you know. You could have agreed to come back home with me earlier and avoided all of this." His fingers brushed the cheek on the uninjured side of her face in a reassuring touch. "And someone, other than you, needs to know how to reach your parents. What if your injuries would have been worse? I had no idea how to contact anyone in your family."

Her dad. Micah sighed. That was the person from her past she longed for at times like this. And at more and more times, it seemed, as the days went by. But she shook her head. "The only call to make would be to Carole."

The straight glance he gave her indicated his displeasure at her answer, but he gave no reply.

"Don't be angry." The words rushed out before Micah was certain she wanted to say them. "Let's not lose any more time arguing over things we can't change."

Rob studied the green gaze that viewed him with tenderness, and he leaned forward to kiss the crown of her head. "Okay," he offered. "Now, you need some rest."

"I am really tired, and I'm teaching tomorrow."

"No, you're not. Liz has already talked to your supervisor, and they've arranged for a substitute for the next few days," he explained as he walked toward the doorway.

"A sub needed to fill in for a sub. I'll bet they loved that dilemma."

"It's not unheard of, you know. Sometimes subs

get sick, too…or, in your case, injured. Now, get some rest. I'll check on you later.''

Micah sank back into the pillow and closed her eyes as Rob shut the door. Sleep sounded good, and that's how she spent most of her day, off and on, except for joining Rob in the living room to eat dinner. Then, unbelievably exhausted, she returned to the bedroom and slept the night away, too.

It felt strange that next morning, being in Rob's apartment and not going to school. It was Monday, and Rob drank some coffee before leaving for the office. Micah poured a second cup and sat down in front of the television to watch the news. The school had given her several days off to recuperate, and she was sore enough to be grateful to sink into the couch and rest. Soon, Grace let herself into the apartment with a spare key Rob had provided. And she wasn't alone. Ashley, her kitten, had come along, too.

"Hi, dear. How are you feeling?" Grace called after letting herself and her pet in. "Sorry I didn't get here earlier, but that traffic was terrible."

"Hi. You brought Ashley?" Micah leaned over to pick up the kitten when she winced as pain shot through her temple.

"Are you all right? Here, don't move around so quickly. You'll hurt yourself more." Grace squeezed Micah's hand affectionately before handing the fluffy visitor to her. "I thought Ashley could stay here for a couple of days to keep you company. I brought everything she needs."

"You don't think Rob will mind?" Micah asked with uncertainty.

"My goodness, no. He won't mind at all. My dear girl, I'm so sorry you were hurt," she said suddenly and touched Micah's face. "Thank the good Lord for sending Rob back up there that night." She gave Micah a gentle hug. "Of course, Rob won't admit that God had anything to do with it."

Micah laughed softly. "That doesn't surprise you, does it?"

"Not at all. But I am hoping that he'll see God bringing something good out of something bad that happened. Your head will heal up nicely, I'm sure…and it has brought you and Rob back together."

A bittersweet smile curved one corner of Micah's lips. "For a while," she replied.

Grace sat down next to Micah on the couch. "I know I'm not supposed to meddle in the affairs of my children, but Rob mentioned your dislike for his work—"

"It's more than that. Honestly, it's more than you want to hear."

"I doubt that, Micah. I'd listen to whatever you wanted to tell me, and I'll accept it if you don't want to tell me anything. But if his work is the biggest stumbling block, you should know that there are other possibilities—"

"No," she interrupted as gently as she could. "Wanting me shouldn't cause him to give up something he's worked very hard to have. I don't want him to become something different than he is because he fell in love with me."

Grace's smile was warm. "People who touch our lives often change us." She paused. "How could he not be different after loving you?"

Micah bit her lower lip so hard it throbbed. How could she ever find the words to let this woman know how much her kindness meant? "I love your son more than I've ever loved anyone. I don't want to hurt him, not in any way."

Grace nodded her head with certainty and leaned forward to give Micah a hug just as Ashley started meowing. Loudly. And they both laughed at the squeaky noise.

"What's wrong, Ashley? Not getting enough attention?" Micah asked while rubbing the kitten under its chin.

"You two seem to have a mutual fondness for each other, so I thought she might brighten your days." Grace stood up and headed for the kitchen. "I've brought sandwiches for lunch. I see you already have the coffee on."

"Rob made it, actually. It's still hot."

"Okay, I think I'll put these in the refrigerator." She opened the door of the appliance. "I don't know why that son of mine doesn't starve to death. There's almost nothing in here. Milk, juice, butter, eggs...."

"He eats out a lot. But I know he cooks occasionally. He made French toast one morning for Angela's kids, and he made supper for us last night.''

"And what did you have?" Grace asked.

"Scrambled eggs and toast."

"Good. Sounds like he's taking pretty good care of you."

Micah smiled. "I wasn't really hungry, anyway. Anything he made would have been fine with me."

Grace shook her head. "You're much too agreeable. Now, let's see what I can start with," Grace said as she searched through the sack of items she'd brought with her. "I'll make chili. I have everything I need with me, and it will give me something to do today while we're talking."

And that's how the day went. They talked, laughed, cooked and baked since Grace had included the ingredients for oatmeal cookies in her bag of goodies. Micah's head still hurt although the pain was lessening, and by late afternoon she felt tired and returned to the bedroom for a nap. When she awakened some time later, Rob was home from the office and Grace had left, leaving Ashley behind.

"A cat," Rob said quietly. "I guess I'd better buy a litter box tonight."

"We already have one. Your mom brought it and some cat food, too."

"Accessories included, huh?" he remarked. "Mom is very thorough."

"She cooked dinner for us. Homemade chili and

fresh oatmeal cookies, your favorite dessert according to her.''

"She's mistaken about that. She must have forgotten to include you in that category.'' Rob clasped the soft hand Micah extended to him.

"Hmmm...apparently so,'' she said with a light laugh. "I don't remember being mentioned in her list of possibilities.''

"That's because you're not part of any list. You *are* the list. Now and always.'' A flash of regret clouded his expression as his mouth thinned into a grim line. Always would never be, and they shared that thought without words.

Micah's head ached more than it had all day, and it was nothing compared to the ache in her heart. But she nodded and attempted a smile. "Let's have dinner before it gets cold.''

Rob squeezed her hand gently and nodded. Together they walked hand in hand to the small table in the kitchen. "Looks good,'' he commented while pulling out a chair for Micah.

"It is good. I've already tasted it. Your mother is a great cook.''

He nodded again but didn't respond. So Micah prayed for their meal and then reached for the iced tea. "How was your day?''

"Not good. I spent nearly two hours working out a separation agreement with a young couple who want out of their marriage.''

Micah studied the frown settling over his expression. "You've handled lots of domestic cases. Why does this one bother you?"

"They've been married for only one year. One year, Micah, and they're calling it quits. Doesn't anybody try anymore?"

"Not everyone goes into marriage with the idea of permanence like Christians. And not all Christian marriages last, either."

"But these two don't need to separate. All they need is some marriage counseling, some forgiveness, and, I don't know, maybe a church life."

"A personal relationship with God is what they need. You know as well as I do that a church life never saved anyone."

"It won't save their souls, but it might help their marriage. Involvement in a good church can be the beginning of them doing something together instead of always insisting on their own way."

Micah hesitated before speaking again. Then she decided to ask what she had asked before without success. "Would you go to church with me this Sunday?"

"Micah, this isn't about me. It's about—"

"It's about your recommending a church life to someone," she answered quietly. "Do as I say and not as I do?"

Rob flashed an irritated glance her way. "Just because I don't always do the right thing doesn't mean I don't know what the right thing is."

"But your counseling is sounding less and less

legal, and more and more of a spiritual nature. I know your heart goes out to these people, but you can't solve everyone's problems. You can really only completely solve your own.''

''I don't have a problem. My life isn't exactly falling apart.''

''Is that what you're basing your need for God on? Must you sink to a certain level before you'll allow Him to pull you up again? Maybe you're too self-sufficient, too strong to let yourself depend on Him.''

Rob's gaze was steady and cold, and the square set of his jaw revealed his irritation even more than the icy blue of his eyes. ''To depend on Him would be to rely…to trust…to be certain of. When I can have those things back, then He can have my life again.''

''But think of how He's helped me. He led you right back to my cabin that night. If you hadn't come back, I don't know how long it would have taken for someone…*anyone* to find me lying there in the rain, bleeding.''

''And what if I hadn't come that night? I almost didn't. I know how stubborn you can be—''

''But you *did*. You came when I needed you, and we have the Lord to thank for that. I know there are a lot of inadequate answers in life. And I know that's what led you away from your Christian beliefs. But I think, in your heart, you want to come back. Listen to yourself. You're finding better answers in God's word than you are in the Ohio Revised Code.''

"He has answers that help some people, but what I see, what I live daily is a life that is better now than it's ever been. And it's not been accomplished with prayer and dependence. Even you—''

"Me?''

"If I'd followed the path I was on, I wouldn't have you. I wouldn't have become a lawyer, wouldn't have met you in my office that day you came in regarding the Winslow accident. I'd have been off in some other community and not at Wellspring Elementary School for Career Day. You and I wouldn't even know each other.''

"And maybe, in the long run, you'd be grateful,'' she stated, her voice deadly quiet.

"Don't start with that, Micah. I don't want to hear about how your dad's run-in with the law is going to destroy my career. I love you, and there's nothing about you that can hurt me so terribly that some day I'll wish I hadn't met you. You're the best thing in my life.''

"I don't want to be the best thing in your life. I want the Lord to be that for you.''

That comment brought a stern-faced expression to his features. Rob rose to his feet and left Micah sitting alone at the table with a dinner they both had lost interest in. He walked to a nearby window and stood, looking out, with his hands in his pockets.

Micah sat silently for a moment, watching him.

She could see his frowning face in profile and wondered why she hadn't noticed before now how worried he looked tonight. "You okay?" she asked softly as she stood up.

He gave her a distracted nod and cleared his throat. "Remember that night at your apartment when you told me it was over? And I got angry and walked out?"

"Yes," she replied, reluctantly recalling that pain.

"Do you remember telling me that 'today' was all you had to give?" He turned his head, glancing at her with an unreadable expression.

"Yes," she said as she approached him. "I remember."

"Well, I want to take your offer."

Micah's eyes widened in surprise. "But…you know that what we've had here can't last—"

"It can last for a while. Until what you fear will happen, begins to happen. And when you say it's time to end, I'll let you go. With no anger."

Her head pounded relentlessly with logic and facts about why this idea was crazy. But, against all her better judgment, her hopes soared. He was right. It could last for a while. They were together, here, tonight, and who could say how many more todays they could share before her past collided with their future? His arms encircled her, bringing her close, holding her near, and she buried her face against his throat.

"Micah, I want you to be my wife."

She raised her head. "Rob, don't—"

His fingers touched her lips, silencing her words. "I won't," he replied. "I won't ask you for something you can't give. But I wanted to say it. I want you to know that I'll always love you."

"I know...and I love you that same way," she admitted as she searched his troubled eyes. "I'm glad I'm here, with you, now."

"So am I," he offered, his voice nearing a whisper as his mouth slowly descended to meet hers in a surprisingly gentle kiss. But the delicious sensations he created did nothing to ease the pain shooting through Micah's bruised temple. It felt very real—not yet the distant memory she longed for it to be—and she involuntarily winced in response.

Rob pulled slightly away from her, enough to look into her eyes. "Your head still hurts, doesn't it?"

"Yes, and I wish it didn't. Not now."

"We probably both wish a lot of things," he commented before kissing her mouth again, gently. "But reality, my love, is what we deal with. And you've had a bad injury. It's gonna take time to heal."

"I'll be all right."

"If you don't feel some significant improvement soon, I want you to see another doctor." Rob touched her cheek lightly. "Get some rest. Mom probably wore you out today, and I have some work to do, anyway. I'm taking a hearing in the morning for Martin, and I need to read over the file.''

"You look so tired. Why isn't Martin handling his own hearing?"

"He won't be in the office tomorrow, so I'm taking care of it. Don't worry about me, Micah. I'm fine."

"Really?" she persisted.

"Yes," he insisted and motioned toward the hallway leading to the bedroom. "Now, go. You're the one who needs some rest."

"First, I'll clear off the table—"

"No. It won't take me five minutes to clean that up. Go on to bed," Rob urged her before turning his attention to the briefcase on the sofa.

"Good night," Micah offered and started down the hallway. Then she stopped and looked over her shoulder at him. "Rob...."

He glanced up from the paperwork at his fingertips.

"I love you," she said openly, honestly—the way she'd longed to say it dozens of times before.

"I love you, too, Micah," came Rob's reassuring response but with a fleeting look of concern that Micah had not expected.

She disappeared into the bedroom to retire for the night but had difficulty falling asleep as she wondered what troubled him so.

The next morning, Rob left early for court and

Grace was sitting in the kitchen drinking coffee when Micah woke up.

"How's the patient?" Grace asked with a smile. "Want some coffee?"

Micah touched her forehead, finding it difficult to believe it was no longer aching. "I feel better today," she answered and reached for a cup. "And coffee sounds wonderful. Rob's gone already?"

"He has an early hearing and several clients to see this morning. He left about an hour ago."

Micah leaned down to rub Ashley's chin while listening to Grace's response. "I'm really feeling much better today. There's no need for you to spend your day watching over me. You probably have a hundred other things you could be doing."

"Actually, I thought I'd clean this apartment. Rob has a weekly cleaning service, but he canceled for this week so they wouldn't be in here disturbing us."

"I'll help—"

"No, my goodness, no. Rob will be irritated enough with me for being too helpful. I'm not going to involve you in this 'crime,' too."

But Micah quickly protested. "I've been useless for days, Grace. It would do me good to accomplish something."

"Well, accomplish something else. Something that won't get me into too much trouble with my son." Grace touched Micah's arm gently with an affectionate pat. "Why don't you paint for a while?

Then, if you don't have anything else to do, you could visit Angela's new home when school is over. It's really beautiful, and she'd been wanting to show it off to you. I can take you, if you don't think you're up to driving yet.''

"I can drive. My head hardly hurts at all this morning," Micah said and with a soft sigh added, "I wish I had felt this way last night." Then she glanced up as it occurred to her how that may have sounded to Rob's mother.

Grace laughed quietly and patted Micah's arm again. "Don't worry, dear. I won't ask." She reached for her coffee cup. "Let's have breakfast, and then get busy."

And they did exactly that. Micah put the finishing touches on her painting of the old Pinewood Church—something she'd been looking forward to completing for a long time—while Grace insisted on working around the apartment, straightening and cleaning, with Ashley under her feet most of the time. Then, late in the afternoon when Grace headed home, Micah took the index card on which Grace had drawn a map to Angela's new address and went for a visit.

Four bedrooms, a country kitchen, living room, dining room, family room, three baths and a den. Angela's new home smelled of cedar and fresh paint as Micah took the grand tour of her friend's new residence. She hadn't been in a house this lovely since her own growing-up days, but this one somehow seemed cleaner, brighter. Maybe because Micah knew this home wasn't paid for with stolen money. As for her own, she wasn't quite sure.

"Rob says things are going very well with the two of you."

"Yes," Micah responded.

"Well enough to last?" Angela asked as a grin brightened her face.

"I wish it would," came Micah's evasive reply.

The two women returned to the starting point of the tour, the kitchen. Then Angela continued their conversation. "I know Rob about as well as anyone does, and I've never seen him in love like this before." She opened the refrigerator. "Iced tea?"

"No, thanks. Do you really mean that? About Rob?"

"Absolutely," Angela stated rather matter-of-factly while pouring one glass of tea. "He needs you, and I can't recall him really needing anyone...ever." She added the last part with emphasis and took a sip of her drink. "So...are you going to stay with him? Live with him?"

"No, Angela, it's not how it looks. I mean...Rob sleeps on the couch."

"Oh, Micah," Angela began with a complete look of surprise registering on her face. "I wasn't trying to pry, and I *certainly* don't want to know anything about my brother's private life. It's just...well, I know he's my brother, but I have to admit he's a nice looking guy, and he's dated lots of women. It seemed like someone different every time I saw him...until you.''

Micah watched Angela struggle with her choice of words, and she wondered where this discussion was headed as she listened.

"But you...you could be forever. I can see that in the way he looks at you. Has he told you yet that he loves you?"

Micah answered wordlessly with a simple nod of her head.

"You know he's away from God right now. I'm talking light-years away from where he needs to be." But Angela's humor was momentary as her brows knit together in a concerned expression. "If you hold that over him, Micah, you could lose him."

"I know," Micah agreed, accepting Angela's insight into her brother's heart. "But he needs to get back to where he was before Nick died."

"He'll never be the same again. When Nicky died that night, some kind of trust...faith...some spark in Rob died with him." Angela stopped talking for a moment, remembering. "That was so long ago, and yet, in some ways, it seems like yesterday. I guess most of us changed in some way after that."

"How, Angela? What did it do to you?" Micah asked.

"I'd always looked up to Rob. You know, 'big brother' and all that kid stuff."

"I think you still look at him that way, and he likes it very much."

"I suppose you're right." Angela slid her hands deep into the pockets of her sweater. "But when he stopped going to church and trusting in God, it had a big impact on me. I became a Christian when I was only eleven and, in the beginning, it was probably more because I loved my brother than because I loved God. But as I got older and understood things better, it became very real and personal to me. I went to Trinity Christian College two years behind Rob and Nicky so I was still there after Rob graduated and Nicky died, and I wasn't nearly as committed to the Lord as I had been years earlier. It was difficult to continue on with something Rob no longer valued. Then I met Dan, and it wasn't long before I married him—even though I was a Christian and he was not. I knew someday I'd be stronger, more committed than I had been, and I thought he'd come around eventually…see things my way."

"But he didn't?" Micah asked softly, studying the pain reflected in her friend's eyes.

"No," Angela shrugged her shoulders and gave a brief, heartsick laugh. "He sees things more his way now than ever before." She paused. "Micah, Dan is a good man and I love him when he's not drinking. But, overall, my Christianity versus his nonbelief is hard on our marriage and on the kids, even during the long dry spells like he's experiencing now. His lawn business is good, he's sober, on the job every day and making plenty of money— and my teaching is going well and my salary is great now that I finished my master's degree—and we can honestly afford this new home…but I'd trade it all for him to become a Christian, attend church with his family, teach our kids about God's love.'' Angela's usually shiny blue eyes flooded with tears, and Micah gently touched her arm in a comforting manner. ''I'm not so sure Rob will ever trust the Lord again, and all I'm trying to say is…be careful. Rob loves you and you love him, but it's not always going to be so simple. Think with your head first, then your heart.''

Micah nodded and tenderly placed an arm around Angela's shoulders, holding her until the tears stopped. And Micah's own heart grew heavy from sad irony. All of the time she'd spent worrying about her effect on Rob's career, she'd barely considered the negative impact he could have on her faith. What a struggle they could face in the years that lie ahead, and how many obstacles could they overcome?

''If you tell my brother I said all of that, I'll deny it,'' Angela stated with a quick smile before she wiped her nose on a tissue. The shine returned slowly to her eyes.

''It's our secret,'' Micah assured her. ''Rob's been so busy at the office, I haven't talked with him much, anyway.''

''That may be just as well. He hasn't been in such

a good mood since Mr. Alsmore gave his commentary on your situation.''

Micah's heart thumped loudly within her breast. She'd heard nothing from Rob about Mr. Alsmore saying anything.

''But don't let it bother you. Rob and Mr. Alsmore haven't seen eye to eye on many issues since Rob joined that firm.''

Micah restrained the questions on the tip of her tongue, waiting for Angela to reveal whatever it was she assumed Micah already knew.

''If you and Rob want to live together, what business is it of Mr. Alsmore's? Imagine the nerve of that man to comment on what Rob does in his private life? I don't even think that's legal.''

Swallowing hard at the growing lump in her throat, Micah placed both hands on the counter beside her. Already the problems were starting, problems Rob had not shared with her—knowing he could not. ''I wonder....'' Micah's mouth felt dry and she swallowed again. ''I wonder how Mr. Alsmore found out?''

''Who knows? Who cares? What gives him the authority to say anything about it? And right on the heels of losing Martin Hanley because of his recent marriage. You'd think he'd learn to keep his opinions to himself rather than risk losing any more good attorneys.''

''I know Martin is one of the lawyers Rob works with because he's mentioned him a few times, but who did he marry? And why did it cost him his job?''

"He got angry and quit after Mr. Alsmore made an unkind remark about his new wife. Martin recently married a woman that he had represented on several shoplifting charges."

"I had no idea," Micah said in astonishment. What else had Rob failed to tell her? How much harm had her presence in his life already done? How much more could it do?

"Angela, I've got to go. Rob will be home soon." And she wanted to pack and be gone somewhere, anywhere, before he arrived.

"I'm sorry you have to leave so soon, but thanks for coming to see the house. Come back when you can stay longer. And say hello to Rob for me," Angela called after Micah as she departed.

Micah forced a smile and waved a goodbye before getting into her car. She wouldn't see Rob to say "hello"...or "goodbye." Anger coursed through her veins on the drive to his apartment. She was angry she had thought that, even for a few days, this could work. Angry she had hurt Rob. Angry she had set herself up for heartache. Again.

After entering his apartment, she haphazardly tossed her clothing and personal items into her suitcase and carried it down to her car. Then she went back upstairs to get her paintings and art supplies. Micah took one last look around, said a sad "goodbye'' to Ashley and left, leaving the extra door key on the table.

She hurried to her car. ''This was never Your plan for me from the beginning,'' she spoke the words aloud. ''I knew it wasn't, but I wanted him anyway. And, now, I have no one to blame but myself. I did this.'' She started toward home, knowing she'd left part of herself behind—with Rob—never to be found again.

When Micah finally opened the door to her own apartment, the place looked clean. And lonely. She knew what she faced now. Days and nights, springs and winters, painting, teaching, the sound of rain hitting the leaves on the apple tree. Would she feel any of it, without him?

She unloaded the car and carried in her suitcase, placing it on the bed. After changing into her old jeans and a faded T-shirt and catching her long hair up into a ponytail, she began unpacking. Suddenly, she remembered leaving some of her paintings on the front step when she had tried to carry too much in at one time. And one of them was her painting of Pinewood, the old country church, a piece of work she was very pleased with when she put the finishing touches on it this morning. She rushed to bring it in before a gust of wind could knock it off the step. She pulled open the front door just in time to see Rob walking up the sidewalk. She inhaled a deep breath and let it out slowly, preparing for an argument and one broken heart—no—two. But anger wasn't what she saw when their eyes met. Some undefinable emotion clouded the stormy blue gaze she loved. And it frightened her.

Rob approached the front door, but made no attempt to enter. He stood silently on the step looking at the paintings leaning against the black hand-railing. Then he looked up, meeting her sorrowful gaze.

"You could have said 'goodbye,'" he offered in an unsteady voice.

"No, I couldn't. Not in person," Micah replied, her eyes already burning with hot tears. "That's the problem."

One corner of Rob's mouth turned up in a sad smile. He blinked, then looked away. "You know that I love you, I need you." His voice was little more than a hoarse whisper, and he spoke without looking back into her eyes.

She nodded, and clearing her throat, managed a quiet response. "I know."

Rob slid one hand into a pocket and with the other he traced the frame of the painting beside him. "I can't think of a better argument than love, Micah. Can you?" He returned his gaze to look fully into her face, studying every feature as though he wanted to memorize it, memorize her.

Micah shrugged and shook her head slowly, loving him so much she could barely speak. "But loving isn't enough," she answered, her words on the edge of a cry. She covered her mouth with her hand.

"I know your concerns about my career. I'm willing to take those risks."

"And I know about Martin and his shoplifting wife. And Alsmore's reaction. And Martin's lost job."

Rob stared down at the step, and scuffed his foot against the concrete. "Liz?"

"She told me, but don't be angry with her. She had no reason to suspect you would keep that from me. She thought I knew all about it."

"Martin's situation is different from ours. Stephanie is a shoplifter. She's already been in court three times on charges—"

"I don't care what she did, Rob. The point is Martin's career with Alsmore is over. Finished. And it's because he married someone he shouldn't have."

"Martin's an adult—he makes his own decisions and this felt right to him," Rob quietly commented.

"And do you think his decision was a good one?" Micah inquired quickly.

"His decision to leave the firm was a good one, the only one he could make under these conditions."

"And his decision to marry Stephanie?"

Rob raked a hand through his dark hair. "I don't know. Maybe in their case, they should have reconsidered. Stephanie's shoplifting is a sickness. I don't know if she'll ever be free of it. It's gonna be a tough road for Martin."

"I'm not going to do that to you," she whispered and turned to shut the door.

"Your paintings," Rob said quietly. "You shouldn't leave them out here like this." He picked up two frames and started to hand them to her through the doorway when he looked closely at the canvas Micah reached for.

"Dear God, Micah. That's Pinewood," he said suddenly.

Micah glanced at her newly finished painting and agreed. "Yes. It's finally done. You recognize that church?"

"Yes. I've been there."

"What were you doing there? It's just a tiny little church stuck out in the woods miles from here. It probably only has about fifty members—"

"And an active missionary council and a crack in the stained glass window at the rear of the sanctuary," Rob finished the description.

Micah's mouth opened in surprise. "How do you know that? I mean, I've been there dozens of times, but you—"

"I made one of the biggest decisions of my life standing in that church," he said in a voice that was deadly calm.

"Did you accept Christ there at Pinewood?"

"No, Micah. That's where I walked away from Him." Rob stared at the piece of art in silence for a moment. "I...I have to go," he stated, his comment spoken so quietly, she barely heard his words.

Then he turned and was gone. And, much to Micah's surprise, her heart kept beating even after he had walked away and left her. Alone. Forever. Without even looking back.

Chapter Twelve

The hot, sticky weather weighed heavily on everyone that Memorial Day weekend. Micah pushed her
damp hair away from her face, and then put the finishing touches on the caricature of a young boy on
a bicycle. The flapping canvas of the tent sheltered
Micah and her squirming model from the full effect
of the sun's heat, and the occasional breeze saved
them from the sweltering humidity.

"Here you go." She smiled at the child who
jumped gratefully from the lawn chair in which he
had been sitting.

"Thanks, lady. Hey, Grandpa! Check this out!"

Micah reached for the lemonade on the table beside her chair. Summer had not officially arrived yet,
but no one seemed to remember in light of the soar-
ing temperatures.

The string of booths and tents, one in which

Micah worked, lined a section of several streets in Chillicothe during this annual festival. Micah had been pleased to find a lemonade stand right next door to her tent. This was the final day of the festival. Although glad for the work and the money, she also needed this distraction to take her mind off Rob, even if it was only a temporary solution. Substitute teaching was coming to an end for the year with only a few days of school remaining, and a season of traveling to various carnivals and art shows awaited her.

After a long, cool drink of lemonade, she returned the paper cup to the wobbly table close to her. Ordinarily, Micah enjoyed the fairs, the traveling, the people. But this year, her heart was not in it. It couldn't be. She had lost it to Rob Granston in the spring. And she wondered if it would ever really belong to her again.

"Daddy? Can the lady draw my picture?"

When the man nodded his permission, Micah smiled and asked the small child her name.

"Mollie," came the reply in a squeaky, little voice. "I'm four years old."

"You're getting to be a big girl, aren't you? Mollie is a pretty name," Micah said as she picked up her supplies. "Tell me what you like to do for fun."

"I'm learning to swim, and I'm doing real good at it," the child responded, wiggling in the chair she had sat down in.

"Okay," Micah replied. "We'll put some water

in this picture. How about a float belt, too? Do you wear one of those?''

"Yep. It's a blue one with three squares. Not two, not one. Three.''

Micah laughed softly at the young girl's precise-ness and began to sketch her, carefully including all three foam squares in the drawing. "I have a good friend named Carole who loves to swim.''

"Me, too!'' Mollie responded, pointing to a skinny girl with blond pigtails and glasses who stood a few feet away with Mollie's father. "That's my Carole. Is yours here today?''

"No,'' Micah answered, glancing at the people passing by. "She said she might come for a while this afternoon, but so far I haven't seen her.''

The girl chatted incessantly from that point on, chewing bubble gum loudly as she spoke. This be-came one of those times when Micah felt relieved to hand the finished product to the customer, receive her five dollars and say goodbye.

The heat had kept many people away from the festivities and Micah noticed the crowd appeared considerably smaller than either of the two previous days. Tugging at her white cotton dress, she freed it from clinging to her legs. If only the rain that had been promised would come. She scooped her hair up in one hand, lifting it away from the back of her neck and enjoyed the lifesaving breeze that skimmed over her.

"Micah.''

Auburn curls tumbled around her shoulders as her head jerked toward the sound of the voice. That's when she saw him, standing at the edge of her tent, looking at her for a long, silent moment with a sadness in his expression she'd not seen before.

"How did you find me?" she asked quietly.

"Carole," he replied.

A woman with a small child entered the tent behind Rob. "Could we have a picture drawn together?"

"She's busy right now, you'll have to come back later," Rob explained as he ushered the woman from the tent.

"You know, don't you?" Micah asked. The fact she had wanted most to keep from him, somehow he knew. She could sense it.

Rob rubbed the back of his neck in a weary movement when he turned to face her. He watched her fumble with a few brushes and pens on the easel ledge, realizing she preferred concentrating on the colorful tools rather than look him in the eyes.

"I came home from California this morning," he acknowledged.

Micah nodded and swallowed hard at the persistent lump in her throat. "And now you know." She raised her eyes to meet his.

This time it was Rob who averted his gaze. But not in the disappointment Micah assumed. He simply could not bear to see the unspoken pain he'd inflict when he confirmed her suspicions. He cleared his throat. "I spoke with your father." Then he met her watery gaze again.

"You had no right," she said hotly.

"Maybe not," he conceded, keeping his emotions in check. "But I had to find someone who would tell me what you wouldn't."

"Couldn't," Micah corrected. "I've never told anyone my father is a murderer. How could I tell you?"

"Micah, you had nothing to do with it. It wasn't your crime."

"But the sins of the father—"

"Belong to the father. That's not just my opinion, it's scriptural. You've done nothing wrong. Let it go."

"I don't know why he did it, and I've never had any of the money he embezzled."

"Did you think I wouldn't believe you? You could have trusted me with this. You know I love you. Nothing will change that. Why can't you believe in my love for you?"

She shook her head sadly. "Because it will hurt so badly when it's gone."

"It will never be gone. Nothing that I've found out changes anything. You could have told me about your dad. You could have told me that your boyfriend back then was a law student. That alone would have explained a lot."

"And I could have told you how Kevin wanted nothing more to do with me once the story was out.

Or maybe I could have told you the cruel comments that he made during his 'exit' speech. Kevin and his parents hated me for connecting him to the scandal. And the thing I keep remembering is how my mother's law practice dwindled to nothing right after Dad's arrest, and she hated him for it. I couldn't bear to think of damaging your career and watching you grow to hate me.''

"Micah, please—''

"What kind of future can an attorney have with the daughter of a convicted criminal? Kevin's parents were right in ending the relationship.''

"His parents aren't to blame. Everyone makes their own decision, and Kevin made his. He was a coward.''

"No, he did the smart thing. His mother warned me that Kevin knew I would only 'tarnish his bright and shining future.'''

"Then, apparently, he was a fool as well as a coward,'' Rob muttered, looking away from the anguish reflected in Micah's eyes. Then he looked back again. "What could be 'bright and shining' about a future without you?''

And Micah smiled. The first real smile she'd given him in such a long time. But it didn't last.

"Rob, please don't make me want you more. This is difficult enough, as it is. Losing Kevin was nothing compared to losing you!'' She spun away from him, moving toward the tent opening to put distance between them.

"Micah, look at me." Rob gripped her shoulders, pulling her back and turning her firmly around to face him. "You're not losing me."

"But, Rob, think about it! My father is guilty of embezzling over half a million dollars, then murdering his business associate to cover up the evidence. Do you want to go through life having a father-in-law who is in *prison?*"

"I talked with your dad for a long time. And I met with his attorneys and read over all the transcripts. He did take the money, but I honestly don't think he's guilty of murdering anyone."

"But there's no way to prove that."

"Probably not. But I'm going to discuss the case with Alsmore."

"No! That will be the end of your job. The moment he finds out who I am—"

"Being a lawyer was Nick's dream, not mine."

"But I thought—"

Rob cut her words short. "I told your dad I want to marry you." Rob studied Micah's wary gaze, disliking the familiar hesitancy he saw there. "He said he could use a good attorney in the family again."

Micah shook her head no. She knew Rob's decisiveness too well. He'd determine to stand by her, to be a better man than Kevin had been, no matter what the cost. "Rob—"

He interrupted her once again. "But I told him you had the feeling that someday you might be a pastor's wife. And I said I thought that would make you happier.''

Micah froze, and swallowed the despair that clawed at her throat. Rob was letting her go. After all the months of telling him he should and hoping that, somehow, he wouldn't, he'd let go. Just like that. Micah wondered if she would die of a shattered heart, right there in that tent on a hot afternoon while life buzzed all around them.

A pastor's wife. She *had* thought that at one time. Hadn't she? Sometime back before she met Rob, back before she fell in love with him…because since that moment, she had wanted no one else. And now it was ending.

Micah nodded and turned from him, choking back a sob. She would let him go, she would get through this. She must. Didn't the Bible promise that ''All things work together for good to them that love God?''

''Micah, what I'm trying to say is that I resigned from Alsmore's firm today.''

''No,'' she moaned and shot a look of disbelief at him. ''You can't! That's your career. That's your life.''

''It's just a profession, Micah, not my life. And it's not the work I've always wanted to do. I didn't even consider going to law school until Nick died. He was the one who wanted to become an attorney, work with his dad. Then he died and, I guess, my faith in God died with him that night.'' Rob raked a hand through his dark hair. "But I'm almost as tired of running from God as I am of you running from me."

"Then stop running. Go back to Him, Rob." Whether or not Micah ever knew a life with Rob didn't change her longing for his return to their faith. She loved him too much to dare think of him never finding his way home.

"I promised Him I would come back when I had reason to trust Him again." Rob's eyes misted with tears, and Micah reached out to him, touching his forearm. "And I've kept my promise." He paused. "Your painting of the church, Micah. I could have been the pastor there at Pinewood when you visited that first Sunday. Remember how you felt drawn to that place and didn't understand why? I could have…should have met you then."

"How? Why?"

"When you saw my diploma in the office, you didn't look at it closely. I told you I went to a Christian college, but what I didn't tell you is that I was a religion major. I planned to go into the ministry, and I interviewed for Pinewood right after graduation…right after Nick died."

"So that's the important decision you made in that church. Not to go into the ministry? I had no idea."

"I didn't want you to know. I didn't want to risk your hoping someday I'd go back to the ministry, because I didn't think I ever would. I thought my life without God was going great. And you...I thought I'd found you all by myself. No help from the Lord. You were a witness to an accident and walked right into my office and into my life. But when I saw your finished painting and realized it was Pinewood, I knew then that God had intended to bring you across my path, one way or another.''

Rob touched her hair, tracing the edge of her ear as he did so. ''Having you...it wasn't my doing. In fact, I'd have met you much sooner, when you first discovered Pinewood, if only I'd been there like I should have been. I'll never understand why God let Nick and Rachel die that night. It still doesn't seem fair to me, it doesn't seem right. But now, for the first time in a long, long time, I do believe He's still working in my life. And I'm going to have enough faith to trust Him to lead me the rest of the way. I have an appointment with the district superintendent next Tuesday to discuss what I need to do to get my credentials reinstated.''

Micah's hand moved to cover Rob's where it lingered close to her ear, and she pressed it against her cheek. His palm felt warm on her face. ''But this means I can't hurt your future.'' Her eyes flooded with tears.

''Now we can both stop running.'' He opened his arms and she came to him, letting him draw her near.

''I love you, Rob.'' She breathed the words against his chest where she'd buried her face near his heart. She held him close. Without regret. With no thought of parting.

Rob kissed the crown of her head tenderly. "And I've loved you since..." He paused, remembering.

"Since I told you Mrs. Winslow drives like a maniac?"

He laughed quietly and shook his head. "Not exactly. I think it happened over pancakes and orange juice." Then his easy smile slowly faded.

Micah raised on tiptoe to brush her lips against his in a feather-soft touch she knew Rob would not settle for. And she was right. He pulled her closer, kissing her the way she wanted to be kissed, holding her the way she needed to be held.

When she could breathe again, words rushed from Micah's heart. "Marry me, Rob, or I'll die right here and now from a broken heart."

"I think," Rob said, then hesitated long enough to brush a kiss against her ear, "that's supposed to be my line." Then he smiled...almost. "So, will you? Marry me?"

"Yes." Micah's arms slid around his neck as she gazed into the gentle blue eyes that touched her soul. "Yes, yes, a thousand times yes."

"You owe me that many after all the no's I've listened to," Rob replied tenderly, quietly. A soft summer shower began to fall, pelting the top of Micah's tent. "I love you, Micah Shepherd, but you'll need to change your name again, you know."

"Paperwork will be easy this time," she responded.

"True. All you'll need is our marriage license," Rob said. "And no multiple-choice selection. 'Granston' is your only option."

"I don't think I ever told you how I chose 'Shepherd,' did I?"

Rob shook his head, his easy smile returning. "So, tell me."

"'The Lord is my shepherd, I shall not want...' After I became a Christian, the Twenty-third Psalm was the first passage of scripture I memorized. And since the Lord is my shepherd and like a father to me, I decided to think of myself as the daughter of a shepherd."

"That's beautiful, Micah," he commented as a seriousness creased his forehead. "You know your Heavenly Father loves you, but your dad does, too. He wants to see you."

"Did he say that, or is it just your opinion?"

"He said it, I'm only delivering the message." Rob touched her cheek gently. "He regrets the past, Micah, and he hasn't been able to reach you to apologize."

"He's the one who told me to change my name and never contact him again. It was his idea." Her words were sharp, but only hurt shone in her eyes.

"He did that to protect you, in case someone thought you had access to the missing money."

"Well, now he can get in touch with me if he chooses. He knows my last name."

"No, he doesn't."

She frowned. "But you said you saw him—"

"I did, but I didn't give him your name or address. You've spent a decade establishing a career, a life with the name Shepherd. I didn't feel I had the right to give that away to the man who made you change it."

"But he knows you now...."

"He doesn't know my last name or even what part of the country I come from, that is, unless he detected that Columbus, Ohio, dialect in my speech." Rob's eyes shone with gentleness. "He's tired, and he's lonely...and he misses you. I told him I'd take you to see him *if* you wanted to go. I don't promise things that aren't mine to give."

A disconcerted look flashed in Micah's gaze as she considered the possibilities. "I don't know if I can do that. See him again after all these years."

"You won't know unless you try," Rob suggested. "He loves you."

When Micah's eyes met Rob's again, they filled with tears. She wiped at them with the back of her hand. "I love him, too," she softly admitted.

"Then tell him, Micah. You are all he has left in this world."

"Yeah, just me and about half a million dollars hidden somewhere."

"I don't think so," Rob said. "I don't know how

much this will upset you, but your father believes that his wife somehow took the money from his accounts and moved out of the country to live a life of luxury. From the things he's told me, I'm inclined to agree with him.''

"Nothing she does could surprise me. She left Dad when he needed her most—''

"And you. You needed her, too, Micah. You were just a kid.''

"I was never the kind of daughter she wanted. I didn't have any interest in studying law or being like her. I wanted to paint and to teach others to paint.''

"That's because you are *exactly* like your mother.''

Micah frowned. ''No, I meant—''

Rob reached for her hand, rubbing the back of it with his thumb while he responded quietly, cautiously, ''I know what you meant, but what you don't know, what your father didn't tell you, is that the mom you grew up with was not your biological mother.''

"Rob?'' She pulled her hand away from him suddenly. ''What are you talking about?''

"Your father's first wife was a beautiful redhead who taught art. She died right after your birth.''

"Died? My mother died?'' Micah repeated in near disbelief with one hand flying to cover a gasp.

Rob nodded. ''Your dad will explain more when he sees you, but, Rita, the mom you grew up with, adopted you when you were about a year old. Everything was fine until she learned she couldn't have a child of her own. Then the criticism and resentment of you started. The distance you've felt from Rita was not your fault."

"I thought all along that my mother didn't love me, that it was my fault. It would have been so much better if they would have told me the truth." Micah returned to Rob's arms, that place of comfort she now knew would always be hers.

"And it would have been better for you to have told me about the murder charges...and the law student."

"I know that now. I'm sorry, Rob. No more secrets. I promise." She smiled up into a gaze filled with tenderness.

"Good," Rob answered as his mouth slanted into the familiar smile that Micah had suspected would be her downfall from the beginning. "I can hardly believe you're really mine. You're so beautiful and lovely and—"

"Yours," Micah added with a boldness his love afforded.

"And no more reluctance about our future, right?" he added.

"None. Ever." She raised up, touching her lips to his. And when the wind shifted, the soft summer rain blew inside their shelter, showering their kiss with its blessing.

Epilogue

"Rob, do you have Sunday's sermon ready yet? I need to add the title to the bulletin I just typed." Micah stepped out the back screen door onto a small patio lined on both sides with red and yellow tulips.

"Not yet," Rob responded, looking up at his wife from where he stood by the back fence. "But I'm working on it."

Micah dried her hands on the dish towel she held and walked toward him. "It looks more like you're working on that gate."

"But I'm thinking all the time I'm hammering," he answered with one corner of his mouth curving into a playful smile. "Quit worrying."

"It's Saturday afternoon. You rarely run this late with a message."

He placed the hammer on the ground and held out a hand, which Micah instinctively reached for, smiling back at him. "Sermons are kind of like manna from heaven," Rob stated. "God will give me this one when I need it."

"And if He doesn't?"

"Sounds like I need to preach a message on faith—to my wife, at least." Rob pulled her gently into his arms. "Don't worry so much. It can't be good for you or the baby."

Micah's hand moved to rest against the abdomen that had yet to show any signs of the child within. "I can hardly wait, Rob. Less than seven months, then we'll see his little face."

"His?" Rob questioned before kissing Micah's forehead and releasing her. He leaned down to retrieve his hammer. "Why are you so sure it's a boy? Just think, Micah, we could have a little girl with your green eyes, all that lovely auburn hair and my plea-bargaining abilities. She'd be able to talk us into *anything.*"

Micah laughed softly. "I don't even like red hair," she admitted, tugging on a long strand of her own curls.

A frown crinkled Micah's forehead. "Plea bargaining. That's the first legal term I've heard you use in a while." Then she asked the question that had weighed heavily on her heart during the past few hectic weeks at the parsonage. "It's been nearly two years, Rob. Are you sure you don't miss it? I mean, the law and everything that goes with it?"

Rob's laugh was quick and sincere. "I miss seventy thousand dollars a year, and the ministry offers me the undeniable opportunity of missing that income all my life.'' But his amusement faded when he glimpsed the concern in his wife's cautious gaze. ''But, no, Micah, I can't imagine ever *missing* being out of the Lord's will. It's a lonely place...in more ways than you can imagine.''

''Thank you,'' she said in little more than a whisper. Then she leaned forward to kiss his cheek lightly.

''For what?''

''For thinking the way you do. I don't know why you love me so, but I'm thankful that you do.''

''I'll love you forever, Micah, for a thousand different reasons.''

She smiled and touched his mouth with her index finger. ''Forever can be a very long time, you know.''

''I'm counting on it,'' he responded and tugged on her hand. ''C'mon. Come inside with me. I'm going to kiss my wife the way I want to...without the neighbors for an audience.''

''Hmm,'' Micah commented. ''Maybe that sermon will have to wait until later.''

''Much later,'' Rob assured her as they walked, together, toward their back door and into the life and the love they would share. Forever.

* * * * *

Dear Reader,

It's a dream come true for me to see my manuscript become my first published book, *The Reluctant Bride*. Creating Micah Shepherd and Rob Granston and allowing their story to unfold was an amazing process, one I loved being involved in, and I am delighted that this story found a home with Steeple Hill's Love Inspired line.

Occasionally someone asks where writers get their ideas, and I don't know the right answer to that question. For me, the characters and their stories seem to somehow find their way into my mind, and I attempt to capture them—their personalities, hopes, heartaches, challenges, faith in the Lord—on paper so that, hopefully, they can find a way into *your* heart.

Happy reading!

Kathryn Alexander